PRIZE
OF A LIFETIME

ESSENCE BESTSELLING AUTHOR

DONNA

HILL

PRIZE
OF A LIFETIME

ARABESQUE®

Recycling programs
for this product may
not exist in your area.

PRIZE OF A LIFETIME

ISBN-13: 978-0-373-83168-5

© 2009 by Donna Hill

www.kimanipress.com

Printed in U.S.A.

To all my readers who have ever dreamed of that one-in-a-million opportunity in love and life, this book is for you!

And to my brand-new grandson, Caylib, who is truly a blessing to us.

Enjoy,

Donna

Special thanks to my ever-patient editor, Glenda Howard, and my intrepid agent, Pattie, for always finding a way to work through my drama, LOL. Thanks, ladies.

Chapter 1

The letter weighed heavily in Sasha Carrington's purse. For two weeks she'd carried it around like a talisman, still not believing the words she'd read over and over at least a dozen times. The only person she'd shared her good fortune with was her best friend, April Harris, and only because it was April who'd insisted that she submit her name and qualifications. Sasha had been reluctant to say the least. *I've never won anything in my life*, she'd groused to herself even as she'd sealed the envelope and dropped it in the mailbox more than five months earlier. Now her future was only a plane ride away, that is, if she could ever get off work, tie up some loose ends and pack her bags.

The instant Sasha spotted Brenda sauntering through the door, she signed off her computer with a swipe of her Summit Hotel identification card. She purposely ignored Brenda's syrupy-sweet greeting which she should have given almost an hour earlier. That was no one's fault but John Ellis, the manager, Sasha inwardly fumed. Brenda got away with murder and John turned a blind eye. Had it been *her* coming into work even ten minutes late, he'd be threatening to write her up.

"Anything I need to know about reservations?" Brenda asked while she settled in behind the counter.

Sasha cut her a look sharp enough to slice glass. "Guess what, I really don't have the time to explain—with you getting here so late and all," she added just loud enough for Carol, the reservationist at the end of the counter to hear.

Brenda flushed momentarily and tossed her head, flipping her very expensive weave over her shoulder. "Fine." She dismissed Sasha with an arched brow, put on her commercial-ready smile and moved into greeting mode as a handsome, well-dressed man approached the desk.

Sasha sighed as she watched Brenda work her usual spell around him, the way she did with every man who came within sniffing distance. His soft brown eyes didn't even register that Sasha was on the same planet. She retrieved her purse from beneath the desk, said goodbye to Carol and pushed through the revolving doors and out into the humid Savannah evening. She adjusted the strap on her purse higher on her shoulder and headed for the parking lot across the street from the four-story hotel.

"Humph, humph, humph," a man who appeared to be in his early thirties murmured as she passed. "Love a sistah with some meat on her bones." He licked his lips like the wolf with Little Red Riding Hood on his plate.

Sasha's stomach flipped when he grinned, baring a row of missing teeth. She shook her head and kept walking, trying not to let the obvious get her down. A fine looking businessman walks into the hotel and doesn't blink in her direction, yet a toothless, my-job-is-to-stand-on-this-corner man gives her a big shout-out. *What is wrong with that picture?* she thought as she deactivated the alarm on her car.

She slid behind the wheel, leaving the door open while she turned the ignition of her ten-year-old Honda Accord in the hope of releasing some of the tightly-packed heat trapped inside. She pressed the button for the air conditioning and inhaled a blast of hot air.

"Damn, it's hot." She pulled open the glove compartment and took out a wad of napkins that she'd collected from her various pit stops. She flipped down the visor mirror and peered at her reflection before dabbing her face. Hmmm, she needed a touch-up—badly. And when was the last time she'd tweezed her brows? She'd all but chewed off her lipstick. No wonder the only catcall she could get was from a toothless hobo. She flipped the mirror back in place.

When the car had sufficiently cooled she closed the door, buckled up and headed for her second job—the family catering business, Carrington Caterers. Between her *real* job at the hotel, the evenings at the family business and the classes two weekends per month for her certification in Hospitality Management and Food Preparation, it was no wonder she looked the way she did. She didn't have a moment to spare for herself, or for anyone else for that matter. Neville, her ex, simply couldn't understand that she wanted more than to spend the rest of her life at the beck and call of someone else, working at something that would never be her own, which was why their ten-month relationship had ground to a halt. She had a plan for herself and she couldn't be distracted by anything or anyone that was not part of her plan.

It was bad enough that she was off target by two

years. By thirty she'd wanted to have finished her advanced degree and have her business off the ground so that she could tell the folks at the Summit Hotel just what they could kiss. Then she could buy that little house she'd had her eye on for almost five years.

In another six months she'd be finished with school and her business plan was almost completed, she mused, feeling mildly placated as she turned onto Charles Street. She zipped through a yellow light and made a right at the next corner.

She truly loved Savannah. She loved the way the late-afternoon sunlight showcased the scenery outside her window. She loved the antebellum architecture, lush greenery, landmark mansions and quaint shops. She was a Southern girl to the bone. She'd been up North a few times—New York specifically—to visit relatives. It was certainly a fabulous place, with nightlife that never seemed to end. But before her week-long visits were over, she was always ready to come home. The hustle and bustle of the Big Apple shaved a good five years off her life. The madmen behind the wheels of yellow cabs, not to mention the ludicrous policy of moving your car from one side of the street to the other on alternate days. She chuckled at the memory of her Aunt Linda jumping out of bed and running outside in her pajamas to move her car in the morning. And the noise never seemed to stop: honking horns, music blasting from car windows and she couldn't imagine that the police and the fire department could possibly be called as often as they were in New York. It was a great city to visit, but she could never live there.

The bright blue-and-gold awning with the double *C* logo for Carrington Caterers loomed ahead. Sasha slowed, eyeing the street for an open parking space, the closer to the front the better. She zipped her midnight-blue Honda into a spot vacated by a gas-guzzling Suburban, beating out a Lexus by a mere bumper.

Sasha bit back a chuckle and kept her eyes straight ahead as the Lexus crawled by her. She could almost feel the cuss words bouncing off her driver's-side window. She turned off the car, gathered her purse and tote bag and went inside as quickly as she could, eager to get out of the sticky heat and into the cool interior of the family domain.

CC had been in business for more than twenty years, starting off in her mother Grace's kitchen on Kennisaw Road where she did "favors" for close friends who were having small gatherings or surprise family events. Grace Carrington's homemade soul-food dinners and desserts became so popular that she outgrew her kitchen and rented the space CC now occupied. Once they were old enough, Sasha and her younger sister, Tristan, helped out. Their dad, Frank, who also knew his way around a stove, handled the books and the deliveries.

Fortunately, the recession had been kind to them. While many businesses in downtown Savannah were suffering or had closed, CC still managed to do well, all things considered, and maintained a profit. Grace firmly believed that food was the best comforter in good times and more so in bad. However, with more people becoming health-conscious and a flurry of government studies on obesity in the U.S., Sasha had been trying to convince her mother and her sister to broaden their menu to include some healthy alternatives. She urged them to serve more than the fried, buttered, gravy-laden, ham-hock-seasoned, sugar-coated foods that CC had built its reputation on. Grace and Tristan were not interested.

Sasha opened the heavy wood door and was greeted by the mouth-watering aroma of CC's famous seasoned collard greens. Her stomach jumped in delight, but she fought back the urge. For the past four months she'd quietly embarked upon a lifestyle change, cutting back or eliminating many of the foods she'd grown up on. It was a struggle, but she was slowly winning the battle, having lost nearly twenty pounds for her efforts. Her mother's high blood pressure, her sister huffing and puffing over the simplest activity, not to mention her Aunt Shelia's heart attack a year earlier had put Sasha on notice. She'd gone from a solid size eighteen to a curvaceous size fourteen. She had plans, and she wanted to be around to see them fulfilled, and if she had to take her mother and her sister with her kicking and screaming, she was going to make sure that they were around to enjoy her success.

"Hey, Charise. My mom around?" Charise was Sasha's first cousin on her mother's side, her Aunt Shelia's daughter. She came in after school to help out a couple of days a week.

Charise was busy on her iPhone. She didn't make a move without it, and she barely glanced up. "In the back." She angled her head toward the kitchen.

"Thanks. How's school?" She patted her cousin's shoulder as she came around the front counter.

"Graduate next year," Charise said, as if by rote.

Sasha smiled, shook her head and walked toward the kitchen. At least Charise was still in school and didn't have an infant on her hip like so many of the young girls in the city.

"Hey, Mom."

Grace looked up for an instant from her task of rolling dough for the crust of her famous peach cobbler. "Hey, baby. Hand me that brown sugar," she said with a slight lift of her double chin.

Sasha did as she was asked to the tune of banging pots and stirring spoons coming from the other side of the wall that divided the baking area from the ovens, supervised by Clyde, the only person who wasn't family that Grace allowed in her kitchen. "Hey, Clyde," she called out.

Clyde poked his head out, his dark brown face gleaming with sweat. He flashed her a toothy grin. "Hey, yourself. How you be?" His eyes rolled up and down her body. "Get any thinner you gone blow away." He chuckled.

"I doubt it," she tossed back. The Hasting women were all "big-boned" as they liked to call themselves. Her mother's sisters, Linda and Shelia, were both double-Ds and size twenty-plus. Her grandmother had been big, too, and Sasha's sister, Tristan, was well on her way to winning top prize. Sasha worried about all of them, but they swore that their men loved it and no one could pay them enough to pass up a good meal.

"So when are you leaving?" her mother asked, not interested in hearing another one of Sasha's lectures on food.

Sasha leaned her hip against the counter. "My flight to Antigua leaves at seven tomorrow night."

"You sure picked a fine time to take off on vacation. You know this is a busy time of year for us, with graduations and weddings," her mother complained as she wiped sweat from her brow with a paper towel.

"I know. But if I don't take my vacation now I won't get a chance to go."

"I still don't know why you have to go to some island."

Sasha had no intention of telling her family the real reason for her trip. If things didn't work out, she didn't want to hear "I told you so."

Sasha went to the sink and washed her hands. She moved next to her mother and began kneading dough for the pies. "I know this is a busy time, Mom," she began, "but this is really important to me."

Her mother turned and looked at her daughter curiously. Her brows drew together. "What's so important about a vacation in Antigua?"

Sasha drew in a breath. "It's just that I've planned this for a while. I can't back out now. This is the first time I've been out of the country." Her voice began to bubble with enthusiasm even as she hoped her mother would share in her excitement.

Grace's full lips were tightly pursed before the glimmer of a smile loosened them. "Be sure to bring me something. And I don't mean a T-shirt," she warned, wagging a rolling pin at Sasha.

The two women laughed.

"I promise I'll do better than a T-shirt." Sasha

rolled out some dough. "Is Tristan stopping by? I was hoping to say goodbye."

Grace shook her head slowly as she poured fresh peaches into the pan. "I sure wish you would talk to your sister. Tristan won't listen to me."

Sasha stopped rolling the dough and looked at her mother. "What happened now?"

"Gary again…staying out until all hours. Won't hardly talk to Tristan. She's making herself crazy, crying all the time." Her mother's heavy chest heaved as she took a breath.

"I'll talk to her. I'll give her a call before I leave."

"Thank you, baby. Don't know what I'd do without you."

Sasha offered a faint smile as they worked side by side. What her mother really meant was that she depended on Sasha for everything, she always had. It was Sasha who had taken care of the house and her younger sister while their parents built the business. Even after Sasha and Tristan were old enough to help out, it was up to Sasha to make sure that Tristan was looked after, got up in time for school, dressed, did her homework, ate and attended her activities.

She must have done a pretty lousy job, Sasha thought, seeing as how Tristan had wound up with a creep like Gary. A part of her felt guilty for leaving, but it was finally time that she did something for herself.

After they'd finished with the pies, Sasha prepared to leave.

"I'll call you before I leave. Okay?" She kissed her mother's cheek. "If I'm not running behind, I'll try to swing by before I go to the airport. I want to see Daddy."

"He wouldn't forgive you if you left without him seeing you first."

"I know. I was hoping he would have been back by now with the deliveries."

"Well, you go on. Just be sure to see him tomorrow. I'll let him know you were here."

"Thanks, Mom. Love you."

"Love you too, sugar." She pulled Sasha into a hug and kissed her forehead. "Be sure to call," she said releasing her.

"I will."

Back inside her car, Sasha had a momentary flash of guilt. What if something happened while she was gone? What if her brother-in-law did something crazy, and she wasn't there to look after her sister? What if her mother's worrying about Tristan made her blood pressure skyrocket even higher? Sasha looked toward the storefront. Maybe her mother was right. Although she didn't come right out and say that Sasha was being selfish, it was implied in her tone and her reference to this being a "busy time." She glanced at her purse on the passenger seat. The letter beckoned her, strengthened her resolve:

Dear Ms. Carrington, Congratulations! The producers of *Heartbreak Hotel* have unanimously selected you for the first-round competition…

Sasha drew in a deep breath, stuck the key in the ignition and pulled out into the light evening traffic. She had things to do. Tomorrow she was going to Antigua!

The moment Sasha stepped through the door of her one-bedroom apartment, she kicked off her shoes and turned on the air-conditioning. Instinctively, she ran her hand over her bulging ponytail that had been struggling to be released from its hair clip all day. She passed by the hall mirror and winced. Her face was framed with a thick halo of damp, unrelaxed hair and the ball at the nape of her neck resembled a mini Afro-puff. Fortunately her hair appointment was for nine in the morning and her stylist had promised that she'd hook her up with a style that would withstand the sun, heat and seawater and even some good loving.

"Humph, this I gotta see," she mumbled peering a bit closer at her reflection.

As she headed for her bedroom she began stripping out of her standard white blouse, navy-blue
skirt and matching pumps. By the time she hit the
threshold she was down to her black lace undies
and feeling cooler by the minute. She tossed her
discarded clothing on the armchair in the corner of
her room. Passing by the full-length mirror that
hung on the back of her bedroom door, Sasha did
a double-take. A smile broke the tight lines of her
mouth as she gazed in appreciation at what her
hard work and discipline had wrought. Her upper
arms, which were once on the verge of "doing the
bird," were firm, with just a soft ripple. Her stomach, which normally had to be held in place by the
strongest body shaper on the market, was flat and
firm, curving out to the swell of her hips—not
much she wanted to do about that—down to her
still thick but tight thighs and dancer's legs. She
unhooked her bra and beamed when her 38Cs
pointed out, not down. Then she turned sideways
and—BAM. Yes, yes, yes! She did the happy
dance all the way into the shower. She couldn't
wait to show off her new and improved self on the
beaches of Antigua.

Chapter 2

"I am so excited for you," April said as the airport came into view. "I know you are going to kick butt." She made the turn into the departure lane. "I wish I could be there with you, but I'm there in spirit."

Sasha and April had met in sixth grade, and for reasons that they could never put their fingers on, they had simply clicked. They complemented each other. Where Sasha was more reserved, April was outgoing and never hesitated to say what was on her mind. Sasha was always "thick," as the saying goes, and April could eat a grown man under the table and never gain an ounce. April was flamboyant and Sasha was understated, preferring to stay in the background. It was April who had always been able to draw Sasha out of her shell, push her when she otherwise would have stood still. She believed in Sasha's dreams and ambitions when not even her own family did. Had it not been for April, Sasha would have never gone through with submitting her application to the Heartbreak Hotel competition.

Sasha glanced at her friend. "I know. My stomach is doing flips. This is the first time I've ever been out of the country, not to mention a contestant on a reality television show."

April patted Sasha's balled-up fist. "You'll be fine. If you didn't have what they were looking for they would have never picked you. The main thing is to have a good time. Enjoy the experience, girl. Getting away from Savannah will do you a world of good no matter what happens. And I'm only a phone call away."

Sasha drew in a deep breath. "Thanks," she said, suddenly doubting the logic of what she was about to do.

"And you look fantastic! Just like the star you're going to be."

April was always good for a pep talk. Whenever Sasha felt down or doubted herself, it was April who reminded her of all of her strengths: great personality, intelligent, ambitious, pretty and a wonderful friend.

"The months in the gym and sticking to my diet have sure made a difference," Sasha had to admit.

"You are going to have dem island boys salivating," April said in a really bad Caribbean accent.

They laughed.

April pulled up behind a white SUV in front of Delta's international departure gate.

"Well, here we are." April turned to Sasha. "Ready?"

"As I will ever be."

They hopped out of the car and took Sasha's luggage from the trunk. She had two suitcases and a carry-on, all loaded with brand-new everything, from undies to beachwear, casual to spectacular, shoes, makeup and accessories. The duo had been shopping for weeks to make sure that whatever the occasion, Sasha would be ready and fierce.

April gathered Sasha in a tight hug. "It's going to be great. Enjoy every minute of it," she said in her friend's ear. "And make sure you keep me posted on your every move. I want to live vicariously."

"I promise."

April signaled for a skycap to help with the bags. "You have all of your important papers, phone and personal items in your carry-on, right? Something to read?"

Sasha nodded.

"Condoms? A smart girl always carries her own."

Sasha blushed. "Yes, ma'am," she said, laughing.

"Good. Well…this is it, girl."

"Did I tell you thank-you?" Sasha said.

April grinned. "About a dozen times."

"I wish you were coming."

"Chile, you gonna meet some fine island man and forget all about me," April teased. "Just remember poor old me when you win that million!"

The friends embraced one last time, fighting back tears with smiles, before Sasha pushed through the revolving doors and was swallowed up amongst the crowd of travelers.

Sasha checked her luggage before moving through the long line of security, and sent up a silent prayer that it would arrive in the same place that she did. After being nearly stripped naked, she put back on her sandals, her jacket, her wristwatch and belt, returned her laptop to her bag and finally emerged into the waiting area. For a while there she'd thought she was going to have to take off her lipstick, too. She pulled her carry-on behind her, hoisted her purse up on her shoulder and went in search of an empty seat, preferably one with a view. There was still an hour to wait before her flight departed and she wanted to be as comfortable as possible.

She spotted three vacant seats in the corner near the check-in counter. Maneuvering around outstretched legs and luggage she made it to the other side of the counter and plopped down in a seat with a sigh of relief. She took a quick look around at the passengers, sizing up who was with whom and who was single, who was on vacation and who was traveling on business. She wondered how many were going all the way to Antigua and how many were getting off at the stopover in Puerto Rico. From what she could tell there was a nice cross-section, but no one that really stuck out. To occupy herself she began making up stories about the passengers, pairing up those who were single, and conjuring up images of the couples and what their lives were like. She checked her watch. A whole ten minutes had gone by. Sighing, she shifted in her seat then dug in her purse for the novel she'd brought with her.

"Anyone sitting here?"

She looked up and her heart jumped in her chest. A chocolate-brown Adonis stood above her, almost a dead ringer for Michael Jordan. "Uh, no."

"Mind if I sit next to you?"

His voice was rich, like maple syrup with a slight drawl, she thought. "Sure. I mean, no," she sputtered nervously.

He smiled and lowered his long, lean body into the seat, spread his thighs and pulled his bag between them.

Sasha zeroed in on her book and tried to concentrate on words that were making no sense over the tantalizing scent of his cologne. Heat pooled at her neck and flooded her face as she watched from the corner of her eye, as his slender fingers tapped against his thigh.

"That's what I should have done," he said.

"Uh?"

He lifted his square chin toward her book. "I should have brought something to read to kill some time."

"Oh," was all she could come up with.

"Are you going all the way to Antigua?"

"Yes. You?"

"Yep. First time?"

"Yes. What about you?"

"I've been there once. Beautiful place." He drew in a breath and she gulped as his broad chest spread beneath his fitted black T-shirt. "Perfect weather, incredible beaches and the people are great. They have their share of poverty, but they try to keep that away from the tourists."

"What brings you back? Business?"

"Something like that. What about you?"

She closed her book and was on the verge of telling him her amazing story, but remembered the clause in her contract. "Vacation."

"Vacation? All alone?"

She wasn't sure if his question was just curiosity or an indictment. "I…decided to be adventurous."

One corner of his full mouth curved upward. "I like that. It takes a lot of courage to travel alone." He paused. "Mitchell Davenport." He stuck out his hand.

"Sasha Carrington." She placed her hand in his and nearly sighed out loud when his warm fingers enveloped her hand, and his soft brown eyes crinkled at the corners.

"I should let you get back to your book. Sorry."

"It's fine. Really." She offered a small smile. *Say something, dummy.* "Do you live in Savannah?"

"Atlanta. I've been thinking of relocating to Savannah. I've been here about a month looking at places."

"It's a big change from the ATL," she teased.

He chuckled and the sound shimmied down her spine. She squeezed her knees together.

"That it is. But I like the slower pace." He paused for a moment. "Tell you what, how about I show you around Antigua, and if we're still speaking to each other, maybe you can show me around Savannah when we get back."

Sasha's mind came to a screeching halt. Were her ears playing tricks on her? Did he actually just tell her he wanted to spend time with her on a Caribbean island?

"Hey, I'm sorry," he said when he got only a

stunned look in lieu of a response. "That was out of line. You don't know me from the man in the moon." He suddenly stood up. "I'm going to go grab something to eat. Nice talking to you. Enjoy your trip."

By the time her mind caught up with what was happening, Mitchell Davenport was three aisles away heading for the food court. She wanted to kick herself and could almost hear April's cries of disbelief ring in her ears. She felt like a complete fool and wished she could disappear. Thankfully, a young couple and their little boy took up the vacant seats next to her. Now she wouldn't have to worry about him coming back to pick up where they'd awkwardly left off. She buried her face in her book. *Great start to my journey,* she silently chided herself and hoped it wasn't an indication of things to come.

Mitchell inched up on the line at Starbucks. *That went well,* he groused to himself, a testament to how his relationship life was going lately. What had he been thinking? That's just it, he hadn't been. He'd spotted Sasha Carrington the instant she'd materialized in the waiting area, and his good sense and his promise to himself to stay away from women flew out the window. She was gorgeous in an understated way, with a body to die for.

She gave off an air of quiet assurance and was apparently unaware of her sensual appeal. He could still smell her soft, alluring scent and hear the way her voice stroked him from the inside out. It was completely out of character for him to trip over himself with a woman he didn't know. But her rebuff had been a solid kick to his ego. It had reinforced his vow to remain focused on what was important: rebuilding his life and his business. Everything else could take a backseat. His ugly and painful breakup with Regina had taught him a major lesson: women don't want a man who is down on his luck, who can't provide for them in the fashion to which they've grown accustomed. He'd been devastated when Regina had told him that it was over at a time when he needed her love and support more than anything. He'd lost his restaurant and the bank had foreclosed on his home. He was struggling every day just to hold his head up, and Regina had decided she couldn't or wouldn't deal with his "issues," as she called them. His manhood was attached to his wallet. And at the moment it was running on empty. But that was going to change, he thought as he paid for his purchase. If Regina did nothing else in the three years that they were together, she had taught him an invaluable lesson—no woman would ever again be able to call his manhood into question.

Mitchell returned to the waiting area and spotted Sasha just as she glanced in his direction. He made a point of walking to the other side of the waiting area to find a seat.

Sasha flinched. The warm, inviting look that she'd seen earlier in his eyes was definitely gone. If it was possible to look through someone, that's exactly what Mitchell just did. *Fine,* she thought. Although it may have been April's agenda for her to find a man—even temporarily—it wasn't hers. Her goal was to win this competition. Period. She settled back in her seat and concentrated on her book. At least she tried to.

Finally the flight was called and boarding began. To Sasha's dismay, Mitchell was seated in the row across the aisle from her, both of them with aisle seats.

"Need some help with that?" came the voice from behind her as she struggled to get her carry-on into the overhead rack.

She schooled her expression and turned around. Her heart fluttered in her chest. He was so close that she could see the light flecks of brown in his eyes. "Y-yes. Please."

He took her heavy bag and lifted it like a loaf of bread, pushing it securely into place.

"Thank you."

"No problem," he said without inflection. He took his seat and fastened his seatbelt, reached into the pocket in front of him and pulled out one of the in-flight magazines.

Sasha followed suit and settled into her seat. The words of her novel danced a jig on the page. She wanted to say something, apologize for acting like a deer in the headlights, but the words wouldn't come.

The stewardess made the routine announcements in preparation for takeoff, and moments later they were in the air. Mitchell put on his headphones, adjusted his seat and closed his eyes. Whatever Sasha may have figured out to say by way of an apology was moot now.

Throughout the three-hour flight Sasha stole sidelong glances at Mitchell. For the most part he had completely tuned her out and the world around him, except for when the flight attendant came through the cabin with refreshments. He took off his headphones and for an instant actually looked at Sasha. She offered a small smile, which he didn't acknowledge. His cold-water-in-the-face dismissal was an unwelcome jolt of reality. It was clear that whatever interest he might have had no longer existed. The flight became unbearably long.

* * *

When they disembarked in Puerto Rico to change planes and claim their luggage, Sasha and Mitchell took great pains to stay out of each other's line of sight as they moved in and out of the crowd. To kill some time, Sasha took a quick stroll through the terminal to hunt for souvenirs. She found a cute T-shirt for April, glass salt-and-pepper shakers for her mother, a baseball cap for her dad and some beautiful hand towels for her sister.

With her stash in hand Sasha returned to the baggage claim area and looked for her bag on the conveyor belt. She felt Mitchell before she actually saw him. With a bit of reluctance she turned to her left, glanced, then looked away. She twisted the plastic bag in her hands and accidentally bumped him when she adjusted her oversize purse on her shoulder.

"Oh, sorry." Her eyes danced everywhere but on his face.

"No problem." He craned his neck over the row of passengers in front of him. "Our bags are probably in the corner over there." He lifted his chin in the direction of a holding area for luggage. "One of the ground crew said the baggage handlers take the bags off and stash them on the side to make room for the next flight. So if you don't see yours now, it's probably over there."

She frowned for an instant at the odd practice. But this wasn't Georgia, she concluded. "Hmm, thanks for the tip. Guess I'd better take a look." She started to move away and felt his eyes behind her. Her heart thudded and her body tingled even as she firmly instructed her hips to sway like the willows of Savannah.

Mitchell nearly collided with another passenger as he became mesmerized by the pendulum swing in front of him. He was still smarting from their last conversation, but for the life of him he couldn't seem to shake Sasha Carrington from his thoughts. Throughout the first leg of the flight, he'd tried to concentrate on the motivational lectures he'd uploaded to his iPod and failed miserably. And, because his ego was bruised, he'd rebuffed her smile—an obvious peace offering—in favor of indifference, a persona that was far from who he really was. But since his breakup with Regina, he wasn't the same man. He knew it. He felt it in the pit of his stomach. His confidence had been shaken. Although they'd parted ways months ago, the wounds were still felt fresh and his trust in women and relationships would take a long time to heal, if ever. With that bit of reality, he pushed thoughts of Regina, Sasha and women in general to the far corners of his mind.

* * *

When they landed at V. C. Bird International Airport in Antigua, Sasha was immediately swept up in a whirlwind of sights, lilting sounds and alluring scents. She, along with the other passengers, were guided through customs and into the waiting area to once again reclaim their luggage. She was amazed at the level of activity at what appeared to be the smallest airport she'd ever seen; customs, baggage claim and the eager drivers who waited outside the airport for would-be fares, were all mere steps from each other.

Amid the throng of moving bodies she'd periodically caught glimpses of Mitchell, but she made it a point not to let her gaze linger. This was probably the last time they would see each other anyway. Gathering her bags, she walked outside into the balmy air of the Caribbean, the heat tempered by the setting sun beyond the horizon. She took the travel information from her purse and looked over the information that had been provided in her letter of agreement. She was staying at the Jolly Beach Resort, and would be a guest there for the duration of her three-week stay, with the actual competition taking place offsite. She tucked the letter back in her purse and followed the crowd toward the waiting vehicles.

Her pulse quickened. Two people ahead of her was Mitchell. The woman who stood between them suddenly began waving at someone who Sasha couldn't see, before darting off into the waiting arms of a man who wrapped her in a tight embrace before kissing her like a man drunk on desire and deprivation.

Sasha lowered her gaze, suddenly feeling like a voyeur as the intimate scene unfolded. The line inched forward and Sasha made a point of keeping an appropriate distance between her and Mitchell. The last thing she wanted to do was bump into him from behind.

A white van pulled up in front of them. Sasha breathed a sigh of relief. He'd get into the van and be on his way. The driver hopped out, dragged a limp handkerchief across his sweaty forehead and shouted, "Jolly Beach!"

Sasha and Mitchell moved in unison toward the waiting ride, bumping hips and luggage in the process. Mitchell looked over his shoulder. Sasha stopped in her tracks.

"Jolly Beach?" he asked. She nodded her response and was jostled by the couple behind her.

"Are you two getting in?" the man asked, his fat brown face glistening in the waning light.

"Room for all," the driver called out. He snatched up Mitchell's bag and loaded it into the back and did the same for Sasha before grabbing the couple's luggage.

The older couple, spry for their age, hurried right past Sasha and Mitchell and secured the seats in the back. Mitchell stepped aside to let Sasha on, helping her up with a firm hand on her arm. A shiver ran up the line of her back and she almost tripped over her own feet. *Real smooth,* she thought, thankful for the dark interior of the van. She scooted across the worn upholstered seat and pinned herself against the window, praying for the driver to hurry and turn on the air conditioning.

Mitchell stooped low to get in and, after assessing the seating arrangements, took the only available seat, the one next to Sasha. He adjusted his solid body, inadvertently bumping his hip against hers. "Sorry," he murmured then folded his arms across the tight expanse of his chest and stared ahead.

Sasha's heart thumped. Sweat trickled down the valley of her breasts as she tried to gather herself into an invisible knot.

The driver hopped in on the right-hand side of the van, put it in gear and took off into the night. The van banged and bumped along the frighteningly narrow roads at death-defying speeds. Sasha's heart hammered along with the banging and rattling, and she was sure that they were going to hurtle into a ditch, never to be seen again. She held on to the armrest for dear life. The one perk to the speed was that it stirred up gusts of air which cooled her body.

The only time the driver slowed was to allow two goats to cross the road. She could barely make out the landscape, but what she did see was not what was advertised in the brochures. Clapboard houses leaning left and right, stray dogs and cats, cows, sheep, and a ragtag complement of residents sitting on rickety steps or strolling along dirt roads.

The tug and pitch of the ride put Sasha and Mitchell in constant bodily contact, sending shock waves rippling up and down her thigh even as she pretended not to notice him or the way his leg felt against hers.

The van suddenly swerved around a double-parked car and Sasha tipped over into Mitchell's lap. For a moment neither one moved or breathed. Alarm lit her eyes and the heat of embarrassment burned her cheeks when she looked up at him staring down at her. And then he smiled and it was sunlight rising over the horizon. She froze at the awesomeness of it.

"We have to stop meeting like this," he teased, his warm voice taking the sting out of her awkward predicament. The van bumped again and she struggled to sit up. "I am so sorry," she said, looking every place but at him.

"I'd rather have you fall in my lap than that one back there," he said in a pseudo whisper with a flick of his head in the direction of the couple behind them.

Sasha giggled.

They were both silent for a moment until Mitchell said, "Hey, why don't we start over? Mitchell Davenport." He extended his hand.

Sasha hesitated but a second before placing her hand in his. "Sasha Carrington." She smiled. "Nice to meet you, Mitchell."

"Since it looks like we'll be staying at the same resort, why don't you call me Mitch? All my friends do."

"Mitch…"

His dark eyes caught flecks of light as they glided over her. She drew in a breath and held it.

The van swerved again. This time Mitchell caught her. They laughed at the absurdity of what was to be their ordeal until they arrived at their destination.

"Do they all drive this way?" she asked, brushing the loose strands of her windswept hair away from her face.

Mitchell chuckled. "Pretty much. You get used to it after a while."

"I'm still freaked out about them driving on the wrong side of the road."

"That does take a bit of getting used to," he agreed. He peered out the window. "It shouldn't be much longer."

Sasha dared to look out the window and noticed that the landscape had decidedly changed. Gone were the ramshackle homes and worn- and weary-looking residents. In their place were rolling green hills, towering palm trees and beautiful mansions tucked into the magnificent mountainsides over-looking sprawling white beaches.

The van turned into a long, winding road, braced on either side by trees and lush greenery surrounded by white gravel and stones. The vehicle slowed as it approached a gate. A guard in a beige uniform stepped out of the small enclosure at the entrance to the gate and approached the driver. He peered inside and asked to see their reservations. Each passenger handed over their documents, which were promptly returned, and the gate slowly swung open.

"They're pretty serious about their security," Sasha said under her breath, tucking her documents back in her purse.

"Jolly Beach is a private resort. There are no walk-ins. If you don't have a confirmed reservation you can't get into the facility," Mitchell explained.

They drove down a path that led to the welcome area of the resort, which was outside, much to Sasha's surprise. The reception desk was couched beneath an archway with seating all around. The area opened out onto paths leading to shops, the bar and the beach.

The driver began unloading bags and Mitchell took out his wallet to give him a tip. Sasha did the same, but Mitchell covered her hand with his. "Don't worry about it," he said quietly.

Sasha couldn't decide whether to reject his courteous gesture or if he saw her as a helpless tourist. When they were out of eyeshot of the others she would repay him. She didn't want him getting the idea that now "she owed him."

They walked up to the reception desk and checked in. They were both given wrist bands that would allow them free meals and use of all the facilities while they were at the resort during the next two weeks.

"Here are your keys," the desk clerk said in a lilting island patois with a hint of a British accent. She gave an actual key to Sasha and Mitchell then handed them a brochure of the resort's amenities and a map and directions for the sprawling resort. "Your rooms are on Mango Lane. Make a left at the exit sign and they are across the short walkway." She smiled brightly, not offering an escort.

"Thanks," Mitchell said then turned to Sasha. "Ready?"

"Sure." Pulling her bag behind her, she followed Mitchell through the darkness, the only illumination coming from the moonlight on the graveled path.

They crossed a short bridge that spanned a pond

and emerged on the other side into a tropical paradise. Palms and brilliantly colored flora greeted them every step of the way, filling the air with a heady aroma. Mitchell looked at the signposts stuck in the gravel. He glanced over his shoulder at Sasha. "It's right up ahead."

They came upon a row of white connected cottages and went up a short flight of stone steps that opened onto another row of connecting rooms.

"I'm in 207," Mitchell said.

Sasha looked at her key tag and was surprised to discover that she was right next door in 206. She swallowed. "206."

"Neighbors." He led the way down the corridor and stopped in front of her door first. "Here you are."

"Here I am," she said inanely.

"Need any help?"

"No, I'm fine. Thanks. You've been very helpful."

He nodded, but didn't move. "Are you going in?"

"Oh," she said, flustered. She stuck the key in the lock, opened the door and flipped on the light.

"Mind if I take a look around? Make sure everything is cool, okay?"

Sasha stepped aside. "Sure."

"Can't be too careful," he said, stepping inside. He walked in, opened the closets, looked in the bathroom and went to the terrace, checking the locks. He turned to her. "Be sure to lock this whenever you leave your room." He drew in a breath and slowly exhaled. "Well…everything looks fine. Uh, guess I need to get out of here so that you can get settled." He moved toward the open door.

"Are you always this…helpful?" Sasha asked with a soft smile, her hand on the frame of the door.

"As the oldest with two younger sisters, my father always insisted that I look out for my mother and my sisters and treat women the way I would my own family." His gaze settled on her for an instant too long. He looked away. "Good night. Rest well."

"You, too. And thanks again."

He nodded and walked out. Slowly she closed and locked the door behind him, and suddenly the brightly colored room seemed incredibly dull without him.

She shook her head to dispel thoughts and images of Mitchell Davenport. What she needed to focus on was unpacking her bags, taking a long, hot shower and settling beneath the covers of the queen-sized bed that was calling out to her.

After unpacking, she closed the drapes on the terrace windows and stripped before heading into the bathroom. The moment she walked in she heard the rush of water coming from the opposite side of the shared wall. *Mitchell's room.* Her mind flooded with images of his tall, lean, muscular brown body glistening beneath the pulsating flow of the rushing water. The bud between her thighs jerked to attention and began to pulse. A soft moan escaped her lips.

It had been months since she'd had sex, and even longer that her needs had actually been fulfilled. No wonder she got turned on by the first decent-looking, -smelling, -talking man she met.

Get it together, girl, she chided herself, turning on the water and wondering if Mitchell would imagine her the same way she'd just imagined him.

She stepped under the steamy spray and using her shower gel, generously lathered her body. Her nipples grew hard and the beat of the water between her legs only intensified the long drought that she'd endured. She let the water push the scented soap off her body as she caressed the heaviness of her breasts wishing that there were hands other than her own giving her pleasure. Her fingers dipped lower, answering the demanding call.

She closed her eyes and Mitchell stood in front of her, holding her close, hard and thick between her trembling thighs, stroking her, nibbling her wet skin, pushing her closer to the edge of ecstasy.

Her body shook from the balls of her feet, charging like an electric current up her thighs, exploding in her center, the intensity weakening her

knees. She shook and moaned as release wound its
way through her.

The pounding of her heart echoed above the
sound of the water. Her eyes blinked open. She was
alone—momentarily satisfied.

Chapter 3

Mitchell rose before the sun. He wished he could say that he'd actually slept. But he didn't. More than once he'd awakened during the night with a hard-on that could cut glass, and he owed his discomfort to Sasha Carrington. Throughout the night he'd envisioned her lush body naked in his bed, on the beach, in the ocean and him doing things to her and her to him that are only talked about on a 900 call. Her soft scent haunted him like an apparition. He'd found himself reaching for her in the throes of tossing and turning in his bed, only to discover that he'd grabbed the downy-soft pillow.

Bleary-eyed, he made his way to the bathroom

and turned on the shower full-blast. Maybe an early-morning jog on the beach would shake off the effects of Sasha he hoped as he stepped under the prickling pellets of icy-cold water.

Donning a sleeveless T-shirt and his jogging shorts, he laced up his sneakers, grabbed a hand towel from the bathroom, draped it around his neck and left for the beach. Walking through the reception area he passed the bar and closed shops and inhaled the aromas of steamed fish, ham, bacon and spices as the kitchen staff prepared to open the breakfast buffet at six.

When he reached the beach, a hint of orange glowed just above the horizon. He had about a half hour before the sun fully rose, and the heat with it. He took off at a slow jog, his only company the seagulls and the ocean that rolled toward the shore.

This was the best time of day, he thought, picking up his pace, those precious moments just before dawn, when stillness and the perfection of nature were at their most beautiful. Nothing was more awesome than watching the magnificence of the sun emerge above the horizon. It was a humbling sight that made you realize how small man really was.

He took the edge of the towel that hung around his neck and wiped his damp face. He'd started jogging about two years ago and found that it was the best way to relieve stress. When things had started falling apart financially and romantically, jogging was the only thing that kept him from walking out into rush-hour traffic and calling it a day. After a good run, things didn't seem quite as dismal.

He reached the part of the beach that led to a bluff of rocks where many of the tour boats docked. He slowed and climbed the rocks until he reached the top then sat down to watch the sun rise. A pathway of orange light spread out over the water, wider and wider as the sun made its ascent, pushing the darkness slowly aside.

Mitchell leaned forward and squinted against the light. He really didn't get enough sleep. Now he was seeing things. But what he was seeing was getting closer instead of vanishing like the hallucination he thought it was. His pulse kicked up a notch as the bikini-clad beauty emerged from the water like a water goddess—warm brown, wet, with curves that could send a man driving right off the edge. She didn't see him, and he wanted it that way so that he could enjoy, for as long as possible, the sweet eye candy that made his mouth water.

It was then that he noticed the blue-and-yellow striped towel stretched out on the beach near the shore. She strolled toward it, tossing her wet hair over her shoulder, her strong thighs rippling as she walked.

Whatever he'd imagined that Sasha would look like naked paled in comparison to what was right in front of him. His jaw clenched when she bent down to retrieve her towel. Straightening, she ran the towel across her wet hair and down her arms as she took in the scenery around her, the beauty of the Caribbean being awakened…and then her gaze fell on him. He saw her quick intake of breath, the sudden rise of her breasts. He stood up and began to climb down. He crossed the sand to where she stood, unmoving.

"Morning. I see you're an early riser, too."

Suddenly self-conscious, she wrapped the towel around her. "I didn't think anyone was out here, so I went for a swim, a habit I picked up when I…" She started to say when she began her campaign to get her weight and health under control, but didn't. Instead she said, "When I need to unwind."

"Great bod—exercise," he stuttered, wanting to kick himself for the near blunder. "I prefer to jog. I've never been a great swimmer."

Now what? she thought, her mind going completely blank, which led to a pregnant pause. "Hmm, how did you sleep?"

"Great," he lied. "You?"

"Like a baby." She smiled. *Like a baby that wakes up every two hours.* "I'm going to head back. I can smell breakfast from here and I'm starving."

"I was thinking the same thing. I'll walk back with you." They walked for a while in silence. "Listen, if you don't have plans for today, my offer to give you a tour still stands."

She turned her head to look at him, making sure he wasn't just making conversation. "Really?"

"Yeah, really."

Her throat went suddenly dry. He still wanted to see her, spend time with her. She wasn't going to screw it up this time. "I'd love to."

His eyes lit up and crinkled at the corners when he smiled. "Great. Let's share breakfast and then we can head out. They have some great sights in St. John's. I think you'll like it."

She bobbed her head. "Okay. Sounds like a plan."

They parted ways in front of their adjoining doorways and promised to be ready in a half hour.

The instant Sasha closed her door she darted to her purse, pulled out her cell phone and prayed that her international service had kicked it. It was going to cost her a small fortune on her next cell phone bill, but it would be worth it.

She punched in April's number, closed her eyes, crossed her fingers and waited as the phone rang and rang. Finally, April's groggy voice came on the line.

"Hello." She sounded as if she'd swallowed sand.

"Wake up! It's me."

"Me who?" April teased, her voice still thick as

she rubbed sleep from her eyes and turned her back to her sleeping lover.

"You know good and damned well who this is," Sasha snapped back. "And tell him to beat it, we need to talk."

"And what makes you think I'm not alone?" she asked in a whisper, sitting up then tiptoeing out into the living room.

"Because if I know you like I know you, right about now you're slipping out of your room so he won't overhear you squealing and hollering when I tell you what I have to tell you."

"Damn, I hate it when you're right." April giggled. "So tell, tell," she urged with the excitement of a child. "Who is he and is he cute?"

"Chile…I don't even know where to begin."

April plopped down on the couch and curled her legs beneath her. "At the beginning, of course. And don't you dare leave anything out."

As Sasha relayed every detail of her trip she hunted through her closet for the perfect breakfast outfit. When she told April how she'd almost blown it at the airport, April lit into her like a flash fire.

"What! How many times do I have to tell you to stop being so stunned when a good-looking man takes an interest in you? You are worth every second of the time they spend with you and then some. Now go 'head and finish your story," she huffed.

Sasha shook her head and rolled her eyes at the sisterly rebuke then continued, bringing April right up to date.

"Wow," April said, dragging the word out. "All that, huh? He sounds fantastic, and it's clear even to Stevie Wonder that he's totally interested in you. And you said he's right next door?"

"Yep."

"Now that's what I call convenient!"

They cracked up laughing.

"So I say, enjoy the moment, girl. You know why you're down there, to snatch the prize of a lifetime, and if you hook something extra along the way…why not enjoy that, too? You're not there looking for a Mr. Forever, just a Mr. Right Now."

Sasha tossed the idea around. What April was saying had merit. She *was* there on a mission, and if she managed to get something extra out of the deal with a very desirable man, then why not?

"So, what are you wearing?" April asked, breaking into Sasha's train of thought.

Sasha had laid out a tangerine-colored sundress in a light gauzy material that delicately swept her ankles. She described her outfit.

"Oh yes, that color looked great on you in the store. How did your micro braids hold up in the water?"

"Great. I wish I had done this ages ago. That

stylist is so good that it looks like a head full of soft, bouncy curls. And I can get it wet, pull it up, down and it springs right back. I love it."

"I'll be sure to tell Kim you said so. Uh-oh, Calvin is calling me. Gotta run. You just have a good time, you hear me? And keep me posted!"

"I will," Sasha said with a grin before hanging up. She tossed the cell phone in her purse, thought about calling her parents but decided to wait until after breakfast. At this time of the morning, her mother would swear that something was wrong and no amount of denying would convince her that some harm hadn't come to her child. She checked her watch. Her eyes widened. She'd spent nearly twenty of her thirty minutes running her mouth with April. Now she had to hurry. At least she had "ready, set, go" hair. That was one thing she needn't worry about.

She darted into the bathroom and took a lightning-fast shower, toweled off and lathered her skin with shea-butter lotion and then a sunscreen before spritzing her bare arms and ankles with insect repellent. That bit of business aside, she quickly brushed her lashes with mascara, put gold hoops in her ears, grabbed a tangerine scrunchie and pulled her hair up into a ponytail. The style elongated her face and accented her cheekbones and wide brown eyes. She examined her reflection, turning left then right, pleased with what she saw. A swipe of deodorant and she was ready to slip into her dress with about three minutes to spare. Just as she was stepping into her white flats, there was a knock on her door. She drew in a breath. It was a pure *Lady Sings the Blues* moment, when Billie Holiday, played by Diana Ross, sees Louis McKay, played by Billie Dee Williams, for the first time. If she'd had a wall behind her, she would have slid down it just like Billie Holiday did. Instead, she gripped the doorknob.

"Hi," she managed to say.

Mitchell, with the sun behind him, looked like a bronze Adonis. His milky-white T-shirt stretched across his broad chest was tucked into a pair of tan linen shorts that reached his knees. The hard muscles in his exposed arms flexed and released as he removed the dark shades from his sweet chocolate-brown eyes and looked at her with a sheepish grin.

"Sorry, I'm starving," he confessed. "Didn't want to go over there without you and let you think I'd left all my manners in Georgia when you found me hunched over a plate."

Sasha tossed her head back and laughed full-out, releasing the sexual tension that bounced back and forth between them. "You know what? That's just what I would have thought— *This man's mama didn't raise him right,"* she said laying on the Southern accent. She smiled. "Let me get my bag and I'll be right with you." She spun around, feeling like she was going out on a first date…and she sort of was doing just that. Her heart thumped.

Mitchell watched her easy grace as she retreated inside the room to retrieve her bag. Why did he have such a thing for this woman whom he barely knew? After he'd left her a half hour earlier he couldn't get ready fast enough so that he could see her again. What he needed to do, and quickly, was think with the head on the top of his neck and get back to the game plan. No distractions. He drew in a breath and straightened as she approached, but when she looked up and smiled at him, he forgot all about the plan.

Chapter 4

On the short stroll across the walkway and through the outdoor reception area, Mitchell and Sasha took in the scenery. The resort was quite magnificent, with stone and stucco structures, lush greenery and brilliant sunshine and white sandy beaches as far as the eye could see.

The resort was slowly coming alive as guests clad in bright colors bursting with floral designs began to emerge. The slow-moving and relaxed atmosphere seemed to have put everyone in a festive mood.

By the time they arrived at the semi-enclosed dining area they were surprised to find many of the seats already filled.

"Guess a lot of folks are hungry early in the morning," Mitchell said in a whisper close to Sasha's ear, placing his hand at the small of her back to guide her to an empty table.

His touch felt like hot coals, and even after he'd taken his hand away and helped her into her seat, Sasha could still feel the heat where his hand had been. She inhaled deeply to steady the sudden racing of her heart. How in the world was she going to pretend to be this worldly woman when a simple look, smile or touch from Mitchell made her insides melt?

Mitchell took his seat opposite Sasha just as a waitress approached. She poured water into their glasses. "The buffet is right around the corner here," she began, her voice sounding like music. "And hot food is at the end. Can I get you juice or coffee?" She looked from Sasha to Mitchell.

"Orange juice for me," Sasha said.

"I'll have the same, and a cup of coffee. Please."

The waitress bobbed her head and walked away.

Mitchell focused on Sasha. "Ready?"

"Yep."

They got up and headed toward the buffet and the unbelievable array of food. It ran the gamut from fresh tropical fruit to cold cereals, French toast, bacon and sausage to made-to-order omelets. And, of course, steamy, seasoned fish.

They strolled along the row of buffet tables, loading food onto their plates and giggling as they added more.

"I think I'm going to need another plate," Mitchell said by the time they reached the omelet station. They were surprised that they both liked the same omelet ingredients—mushrooms, cheddar cheese, green and red peppers and spinach.

Balancing two plates each, they returned to their table to find that the juice and coffee had arrived.

"This *is* a lot of food," Sasha said, rethinking her decision to get so much food. She'd been so good about how much she ate over the past few months, and she didn't want to fall back into bad habits. She'd managed to stay away from meat and chosen fish instead, with plenty of fruit. Satisfied that she'd stuck with her healthy choices, albeit a lot of them, she lowered her head and quietly said grace. She was pleased when she looked up and saw that Mitchell was doing the same thing.

"So…" he began as he cut into his omelet "…what do you do back in Savannah?"

"By day, I'm a reservationist at the Summit Hotel. On the nights that I'm not in school, I help out at the family restaurant-slash-catering business."

His brows rose in appreciation as he slowly chewed his food. "You're a busy lady."

She chuckled. "That I am."

"What are you studying in school?"

She told him about the classes she was taking and her goal to one day run her own small resort. "I'm planning to be finished with my degree and certification in a few months. It's been a long haul."

"You're definitely determined *and* focused. Sounds like you really needed this vacation."

She sighed deeply. "It's been so long since I've had a chance to get away." She looked around at her beautiful surroundings. "This is certainly what the doctor ordered."

"Then I'm more determined than ever to make sure you have the time of your life. It'll hold you over until your next big getaway."

She dared to look into his eyes and her breath caught in her chest. The look in his eyes bored down into her center and stroked her, like a feather brushing across the skin, tantalizing and teasing, making her shiver in response.

He squinted. "Cold?"

She laughed nervously. "No." She looked away and focused on her food. "What about you? What do you do in your other life besides squire novice tourists around Caribbean islands?"

He lifted his coffee cup to his lips and took a long sip, stalling for time. The minute he told her what a failure his life had turned into, she would do exactly what Regina had done, slam the door in his face. No woman wanted a man who was down on his luck, especially someone you were trying to impress.

"I'm your average businessman, looking for opportunities in these tough times. I thought I'd see what the investment possibilities were here," he offered casually, just short of the truth.

Sasha chewed slowly, taking him in. "Did you get hit by the economy back home? So many people have been hurt, friends of mine, others that I know. I'm hoping things turn around soon. No one deserves what has happened to them through no fault of their own." She put down her fork. "I know what it's like to struggle and work for something and then have it all taken away from you." She thought about her brother-in-law, Gary, who'd been out of work for nearly a year. It was taking a major toll on the marriage and especially on her sister, Tristan. He was a jerk before he'd lost his job, but being unemployed only made him worse.

"Do you?" He knew he sounded harsher than he intended, but his financial woes were a sore spot with him.

Sasha flinched. "Oh…sorry."

He blew out a breath. "No, *I'm* sorry. I didn't mean to snap. I know some folks that have been hit really hard, too. Friends."

Sasha slowly nodded. "I totally understand."

The waitress stopped by and refilled their beverages. "It's rough all around. We have to support each other. As my grandmother always said, 'There but for the grace of God go I.'"

Mitchell studied her for a moment, wanting to believe that her grandmother's words of wisdom remained fixed in her soul. But what difference did it make? he reasoned. This was all just temporary. They were simply two people sharing some time together on vacation and nothing more. It didn't matter one way or the other what she thought.

"When was the last time you were here?" Sasha asked as she sipped her juice.

"Hmmm, about three years ago." He'd come with Regina, when things were good. They'd been so happy. He glanced away for a moment then focused on Sasha. "You mentioned that your parents had a restaurant. What kind?"

"Soul food. Is there any other kind in the South?" she joked. She told him the story of her mother starting off in the kitchen of their home before taking the leap and opening up Carrington's. "It's actually more catering than sit-down dining. We have walk-ins that get takeout food. But the majority of our business is catering events. And there's always something going on in Savannah." She chuckled.

"It must run in the blood if it's what you see yourself doing, too."

"I have my own version." Her eyes lit up and she leaned closer, resting her arms on the table. "What I want is a small resort, with a full-range of spa facilities for people who want to get their minds and bodies under control. It would offer massages, relaxation techniques, a healthy menu, all in a beautiful environment," she ended wistfully. "That's why I've been working so hard for the past couple of years. I know I can do this. And now that…"

"That what?"

"Uh, now that I'm almost finished school and have my credit in order I can move toward my dream. If the financial market will cooperate," she added.

"A grim reality for all of us. Even if you have some funding, the experience and the will, banks are still scared to lend."

She nodded in agreement. "It makes it harder, but not impossible," she said with conviction. She looked deep into his eyes. "When you sincerely believe in something or someone, you can't let anything shake that belief. All any of us need is that vote of confidence, that person that can say 'I got your back.'" She angled her head to the side. "Know what I mean?"

"Yeah…I think I do." Watching her as she finished her meal, he began to see her in a new and appealing light. She wasn't just pretty, with a knockout body, she was thoughtful, ambitious, and she had a sense of loyalty and a level of respect for others. A far cry from Regina, who only thought of herself, her needs and how quickly they could be met.

Sasha pushed her plate aside, sighed and wiped her mouth. "I can't eat another bite. That was delicious. Now I really do need a swim to work off all this food."

Mitchell had a flashback of her emerging out of the ocean in that bikini and inadvertently knocked over the balance of his water.

"Oh!" Sasha grabbed a napkin and mopped up the small spill. "Did it get on you?"

"No. I'm good." He righted the glass. "Getting clumsy in my old age."

"I think I have you beat on the clumsy thing. I knock something over or bang my knee at least once per week," she said laughing.

"I find that hard to believe."

She grinned. "Believe it, and stand clear when I'm around anything liquid or any immoveable objects."

Mitchell chuckled as he pushed back from his seat then came around to help her up. "I'll keep that in mind." He was so close he felt the warmth of her body radiate from her beautiful bare shoulders. The sudden, hard rise in his shorts took him by surprise, and he quickly stepped back before Sasha did in case she bumped into *his* immovable object. He stuck his hands in his pockets, thankful that his shorts were not form-fitting, and told himself to think about ice cubes. He walked behind her as she led them out.

"I want to make a quick stop in the gift shop," Sasha said, slowing her steps and turning behind her to look at Mitchell. "I packed everything I could think of besides sunglasses." She pointed to his pair hooked onto the collar of his T-shirt. "Be right back." She pushed through the door, setting off the tinkling of wind chimes.

Mitchell drew in a long, deep breath, turning his back to the store. What in the world was wrong with him? She hadn't given him any indication that she was even remotely interested in him sexually, and yet every time he was within eyesight of her he got a major hard-on. If it was just about sex, he'd simply make his move, knock it out and be on his way. But as much as he tried to tell himself that this was no more than an island fling, he actually liked her.

It wasn't just her banging body that turned him on. It was everything—her smile, the way she walked, her eyes, how she was thoughtful, funny, smart and determined. All that stacked up to what could be a problem. And that harsh reality was messing with his head.

Sasha walked through the aisles, needing a few minutes to get herself together. She didn't need sunglasses any more than she needed a tan. But she needed to get some quick space between her and Mitchell so that she could think. As she walked she felt the dampness in her panties that had nothing to do with the island heat. Her clit was hard and throbbing, aching to be touched. When he'd stood behind her to help her out of her seat and she'd inhaled his scent, felt his hands on her arms and his body inches from hers, desire had pooled between her thighs.

If she was a different kind of woman she would ask him to come to her room, strip him naked and jump his bones. And she'd ride him until he put out the fire that continued to rage within her.

"Oh Lawd," she mumbled, fanning herself. .

"Can I help you?"

Sasha spun around, startled by the voice suddenly behind her. "Oh…um, I was looking for…lip gloss."

"Right up front at the counter."

"Thank you." She followed the store clerk to the register, paid for her purchase and stepped back outside.

Mitchell had his back to her but turned at the sound of the chimes. Their gazes connected and seemed to convey the same thing: *I want you.*

"Find what you were looking for?" he asked.

"Yes, I mean no." She sputtered a laugh. "Once I got in there I remembered that I'd packed my sunglasses in my carry-on." She lifted the tube of lip gloss. "Got this instead. So, um, I'm going to dart over to my room and grab my glasses then I'll be ready to go."

"Sure. I'll meet you in front of reservations in the lounge area."

"Great. Be right back." She hurried off, leaving him standing in her wake, and went directly to her room.

Once inside she locked the door, went to the bathroom and ran cold water on a washcloth. She stripped out of her panties, dropping them to the floor, and pressed the cool compress between her thighs. Her eyes fluttered closed as she exhaled a sigh of relief. The cool water slowly vanquished the fever.

Sasha opened her eyes and stared at her flushed expression in the mirror. Maybe the thing to do was stay as far away from Mitchell as possible until this trip was over. Her nipples tingled. "Don't think so."

She went into the next room and took a fresh pair of panties from the drawer, slipped them on, grabbed her sunglasses and headed back out. On the walk over to the reception area, she resigned herself to the inevitable. She was *going* to sleep with Mitchell Davenport. End of story. And once she'd ended her mental and physical tug of war she suddenly felt so much better.

* * *

While Sasha slipped away to her room, Mitchell took the time to try to put this crazy thing that was going on with him in perspective. He was totally taken with her, but he didn't have a pot to piss in. He'd come to Antigua for one reason only and it wasn't Sasha Carrington, yet he couldn't stop thinking about her. She didn't seem interested in him, but he wanted her to the point of physically aching for her every time she was near him. He wouldn't be distracted from his goal, no matter what, but he was *going* to sleep with her. End of story. How's that for perspective?

Chapter 5

The skyline of St. John's, the capital of Antigua, was dominated by the white baroque towers of St. John's Cathedral. Bright, candy-colored architecture dotted the narrow roads like sprinkles on an ice cream cone, giving the entire atmosphere a feeling of carefree frivolity.

The streets teemed with people, both locals and tourists, meandering in and out of shops and eateries.

Sasha and Mitchell merged with the crowds taking in the sights, sounds and smells, and when they were repeatedly cut off by passersby, Mitchell took her hand.

"Don't want to lose you," he said, and her heart nearly stopped.

His hand tightened around hers and everything seemed to disappear except for the two of them. They bumped hips and thighs as they walked and laughed, stopping in the open-air market to sample island fruit before moving on toward the Museum of Antigua and Barbuda.

Mitchell opened the door to the museum, which was housed in the circa-1750 Colonial Courthouse, and they were immediately enveloped in the cool oasis of the space.

"It's not the High Museum," Mitchell said, referring to the museum in Atlanta, "but it paints a great picture of the island and its history."

The museum held an array of fascinating exhibits—from diagrams of the island's formative volcano to displays of local cuisine, from cassava-preparation techniques to the amazing shells whose abundance made them a ready medium for artists. There was a replica of a sugar plantation along with the history of slavery on the island and emancipation as well as the actual bat used by Viv Richards, the national cricket hero.

"These are beautiful," Sasha said, her voice almost reverent as she examined shells crafted into unique pieces of jewelry.

"Pretty amazing," he said softly, watching her

and thinking that the sparkling beauty of the shells paled in comparison to her.

They wandered around some more before going back out into the early-afternoon sun.

"That was great," Sasha said, bobbing her head as she slid her sunglasses up on her nose. "Thanks."

"It gives a pretty good history of the island. The replica of the sugar plantation was pretty humbling."

"Yes," she said in slow agreement. "It's amazing how the Antiguans were able to establish, build and maintain the roots of their culture for generations."

"It's refreshing to meet a woman you can talk to about issues beyond 'Where are we going for dinner?'" he said.

Sasha glanced at him. "So are you saying you just like me for my mind?"

The corner of his full mouth curved slightly upward and his voice lowered an octave. "I'd say I like you for your mind and everything that comes along with it."

Warmth rushed through her and her stomach fluttered. Their gazes held for a moment, communicating things they weren't quite ready to say but definitely felt.

He took her hand. "Come on, let's grab some lunch. I know this great outdoor café a few blocks away."

* * *

Sasha and Mitchell spent the rest of the afternoon talking about everything, from the books they loved, to movies, politics, religion and relationships.

She learned that Mitchell actually grew up on the south side of Chicago. His father worked for the post office and his mother was a nurse. They'd struggled, never had much, but he and his sisters had a good life. He grew up appreciating hard work and what it brought you. He wasn't particularly religious, but he did believe in a higher power and that you reaped what you sowed.

"Church was always a major part of our life growing up," Sasha offered. "I still remember the smell of the hot comb and pressing cream that my mother used every Saturday night to get me and my sister, Tristan, presentable for church," she said, laughing at the memory. "And she'd always tie these big satin bows in our hair. If a strong wind came by we could take right off!"

Mitchell tossed his head back and laughed. "I remember, I remember. My sister used to holler every time my mother broke out that straightening comb. She wore those ribbons, too, and patent leather shoes that my father would shine with Vaseline."

Sasha doubled over with laughter, and slapped her thigh. "Yes! Yes!"

They both hooted at the memories of the hysterical images.

"Whew," Sasha said, wiping a tear from the corner of her eye. "Those were the days."

"Yes, they were." He casually slipped his arm around her shoulder as they continued to walk.

Sasha held her breath for an instant then slowly relaxed under the comforting weight of his arm, fitting perfectly along the contours of his body.

"Have any plans for this evening?" Mitchell asked as they drew closer to the resort.

"Hmmm, no, not really. I need to make some calls, that's about it."

"How 'bout we take a boat ride? The mountainsides are pretty spectacular from the water."

"Sure. I'd love to."

"They serve dinner on deck, music…"

"Can't wait."

He swallowed over the sudden tightness in his throat. "Neither can I." He walked her to her door. "Bring something for your shoulders. It can get a bit breezy on the water."

She wanted to tell him that she'd prefer his arms, but instead she said, "Good idea. Thanks."

"So I'll knock on your door about seven. We'll catch a ride from the drivers up front. The boat takes off at eight-thirty."

She nodded. "I'll be ready." She stuck her key in the door and opened it before turning back to look up into his eyes. "Thanks for a great day," she said breathlessly.

He reached out and tucked a loose strand of hair behind her right ear. "See you later." He went into his room.

The instant she was behind closed doors she spun around in a circle of delight before flopping down faceup on the bed. She couldn't stop smiling. Her insides were beaming. She rolled over, reached for her purse and took out her cell phone. A call to her family was long overdue and the last thing she wanted was to get a call from home at the wrong time. She dialed the restaurant, knowing that's where she would find her mother. With any luck, her father and sister would be there too, and she could fulfill her obligations in one fell swoop.

The phone rang several times while Sasha replayed her day with Mitchell.

It took her mother shouting, "Hello," into the phone to snap Sasha from her daydream. She sprang up on the bed. "Hey, Mom. How are you?"

"It's about time you called. I was getting worried."

"Everything is fine. The hotel is great, the weather is perfect and I'm finding my way around the island."

Her mother huffed. "Still don't see why you had to go so far."

"Ma…please…" She paused a moment, refusing to let her mother's negativity wear away her joy. "How're Dad and Tristan?"

"Your dad is fine. Out making deliveries. And you can ask your sister how she is. Hold on."

Sasha listened to some shuffling and muffled voices before Tristan finally took the phone.

"Hey, sis," Tristan said.

"Hi. How are you?"

Sasha heard the moment of hesitation. "Tris… what is it?" Her heart pounded.

"I moved back home."

"What?"

"Last night. We…I came home and started fixing dinner…he came in and one thing just led to another. Next thing I know he was telling me how much I disgust him." Her voice cracked. "How I'm not the woman he married, that I'm fat and undesirable."

Sasha wanted to remind her sister that she'd been telling her for more than a year that she needed to get herself together, that she was letting herself go. Her husband always had been a creep and didn't need a reason to do something like this. But Sasha would never tell Tristan, "I told you so." That wasn't what she needed to hear.

Sasha drew in a breath and exhaled slowly. "Look, sis, I know it doesn't seem like it now, but everything is going to be all right. *You* are going to be all right."

She heard Tristan's soft sobs and her heart broke, wishing that she could be there to put her arms around her sister.

Tristan sniffed. "I'm sorry. You don't need to hear my troubles when you're on vacation."

"It's okay. We're family. And we'll get through this."

"I'll be okay, like you said. Look, you enjoy yourself. I'll see you when you get back."

"I'll catch the next flight."

"No! Don't you dare. This is your time. I'll be fine. I promise."

"Are you sure?"

"Yes. Now go and have a good time. And take pictures," she added, trying to inject cheer into her voice.

"I'll call you tomorrow."

"Okay."

With a heavy heart, Sasha disconnected the call. For several moments she sat on the side of the bed, hearing the hurt in her sister's voice, the need that she refused to ask for. As Sasha replayed the conversation, she suddenly realized it was the first time that she recalled Tristan ever being the strong one, not falling apart and expecting everyone else to pick up the pieces for her.

In their years growing up, it had always been Sasha who had to be the big girl, set the example, taken care of her little sister. Everyone depended on her, expected her to fix everything—to the exclusion of her own happiness.

She wasn't sure if she was relieved or disappointed that the role she'd held within the family was no longer necessary.

Her cell phone rang. She snatched it up from the bed and looked at the number on the illuminated display, surprised that it wasn't her sister calling to say she'd changed her mind and wanted her to come home. It was April.

"Hello."

"You could sound happier to hear from me. Busy?"

"No. Just got off the phone with my mother and sister."

"Oooh," April moaned, knowing how Sasha's family stressed her out with their demands. It was one of the main reasons that April had really pressed Sasha to enter the competition and do something for herself. "What happened?"

Sasha recapped the conversation.

"She's better off without him," April said without flinching. "I never liked him anyway."

"I feel the same way, but I didn't tell her that."

April was quiet for a moment then said, "If I didn't know better, I'd say you sound more disappointed than upset."

It always amazed her how April could read her moods even when they weren't in the same space.

Sasha sighed, trying to gather her thoughts to explain her ambivalent emotions. "She didn't need me," she said finally. "She didn't ask me to come home, she didn't ask for my advice. She just told me to have a good time."

"And that's a bad thing?" April asked with a tinge of sarcasm.

"No. I mean… It's that I've always been the go-to girl. And as much as I claimed to hate the role there was a part of me that relished it," she confessed, surprising herself.

"I know it's a tough position to be in. You and Tristan are close. You were pretty much her mom most of her life while your parents built the business. But now you have to cut the apron strings and let Tristan stand on her own, or she never will," April said softly.

"I know. I guess I didn't expect it."

"She'll be fine once she gets through this. And you'll be there for her as you always are, just in a different way."

"You're right," Sasha said, drawing a deep breath.

"So other than Carrington drama, how is the trip going?"

Sasha immediately brightened, and spewed out in a gush of giddy excitement the day she'd had with Mitchell and their plans for the night ahead.

"Whoa! Can you see me over here grinning like a fool?" April said over her laughter. "You go, girl."

Sasha giggled and stretched out on the bed, cradling the phone between her shoulder and her ear.

"There is something about him, April, I can't explain it. Every time he looks at me or touches me, I get all hot and wet." She told her about the panty episode that morning, to which April laughed until Sasha had to stop her.

"Whew…have mercy," April huffed, coughing and laughing, trying to pull herself together. "Sounds to me like you have yourself a serious case of lust," she snickered.

"That I know," Sasha agreed. Then, more seriously, she added, "But it's more than that. We connect. We talk. We laugh. We actually enjoy each other's company, and when he looks at me, I feel as if he is really seeing me. Me, Sasha Carrington."

"Dayum, girl, he got a brother?"

"Come on, April, be serious."

"I am! No, but for real, he sounds great." She paused. "All I have to say is this—don't read more into it than what's really there. Folks get caught up and enchanted on vacation all the time. I know you, beneath all those smarts and ambition you are a romantic at heart. You want the knight in shining armor, two point five kids and the white picket fence. He may be the one, he may not. While you're there, test the waters. If it's meant to be, you said he lives in Atlanta…"

Sasha took a mini daydream imagining a relationship with Mitchell back on familiar territory, with the push and pull of everyday life tugging at them both. She wanted to take the chance.

"So, are you bringing him back to your place or are you going to his?" April asked, breaking into her thoughts.

"Oh." She frowned. "I hadn't thought about it. Does it matter?"

"You're damn right it does. If he comes to your room and it doesn't work out, you have to get him out. If you go to his room, you can leave gracefully or stay. Plus you don't want to be in a position of having to ask him to leave, know what I mean?"

"Hmmm, I guess you're right."

"Of course I am. Plus you can see how he lives to a degree. Is he a slob? Neat? Somewhere in between? You can tell a lot about a person by how they keep their space, even in a hotel."

"Good point. Gee, a lot to think about."

"Don't overthink like you do with everything," her friend teased. "Let your instincts guide you. They're better than radar."

Sasha chuckled. "Yes, ma'am."

"Let me let you go so you can get ready. Have a ball. And I mean that in the nicest of ways."

Sasha howled. "Girl, you are awful."

"That's why you love me. Enjoy."

Sasha spent the next half hour laying out every outfit she'd brought with her on the trip. She didn't want to be too provocative but not too provincial either. Sexy but understated was her goal.

She finally decided on a teal-blue, slightly fitted, sleeveless, strapless shift dress that reached just above her knees with a wide matching belt at the waist. The color was nearly identical to the incredible ocean that surrounded them. She had a lightweight shawl in a soft eggshell color to throw over her shoulders.

Rifling through her underwear, she was very thankful that she'd let April drag her through Victoria's Secret to do a complete overhaul from her traditional comfy bras and panties to runway-model spectacular. The moment she slipped into the barely-there underthings in sparkling colors and silky fabrics, she immediately felt decadently sexy. It was equivalent to walking around with your own little secret smile. She picked a teal thong and a matching strapless lace bra and placed them on the bed on top of her outfit, then began putting the rest of her clothes away.

With that task out of the way, she took a shower and a short nap. She intended to be wide awake and ready for the rest of the evening.

Chapter 6

Mitchell had been pacing the floor of his room for the past twenty minutes. He'd been ready for more than an hour, anxious to begin his evening with Sasha. More than once he'd started to go over and knock on her door, but good sense won out. He didn't need to come off as some over-eager hound.

He wanted the evening to be perfect. And if the weather was any indication it was well on its way there. The heat of earlier had cooled to a warm, sultry breeze, perfect for a night out under the stars.

He could almost feel Sasha in his arms as they danced beneath the moonlight, the gentle sway of the ship rocking them back and forth to the rhythm of a sultry Caribbean beat.

He sighed heavily, slung his hands into the pockets of his cream-colored linen slacks and went to the terrace doors. He slid them open and stepped out onto the balcony that was protected on either side, giving each guest a sense of privacy. His view opened right onto the beach, beyond a short copse of palm trees. From his vantage point, he watched the evening revelers as they frolicked on the sandy shores, stretched out on multicolored blankets or diving into the rolling waves.

An image of Sasha as she had emerged from the water that morning flashed through his head and stirred a groan. If he danced with Sasha tonight, he would be hard-pressed to keep his body under control. That he knew for sure. And as much as he didn't want her to think that he was an oversexed guy on the make, he did want her to know how much he desired her. At this point, he could barely think of anything else. His mind was awash with visions of her, the feel and smell of her, to the point of distraction.

He turned away from the scene below and shut the glass doors behind him. He snatched up his jacket from the bed and stalked toward the door, ready to put an end to his physical torment.

He tugged the door open and they both jumped back in surprise.

Sasha's hand flew to her chest.

They both spoke at once, stuttering over the same words… "I couldn't wait any longer."

"What?"

"Huh?"

Mitchell laughed nervously. "You first."

Her lashes fluttered. "I…I was ready. So I thought I'd…well, here I am."

"And I was on my way to you."

"Were you?" she said softly.

He watched the pulse beat in her throat and fought down the urge not to touch her there.

Mitchell stepped closer. "Yes. I was."

Her mouth opened ever so slightly, but she didn't speak. The moment of decision hung between them.

Mitchell swallowed. "Guess we can go, then." He locked his door and stepped out into the night. "You look great."

She glanced up at him as they walked toward the entrance. "Thanks. So do you."

"Get any rest?"

"Not really. Made some calls and spent the rest of the time figuring out what to wear."

"Time spent well," he said, admiring her again.

Sasha felt her body flush and was thankful for the cover of night.

When they arrived at the entrance several vans were already lined up and beginning to fill with passengers.

Mitchell inquired which one was heading for the bay then ushered Sasha aboard. They settled in the middle row.

"At least this one is air-conditioned," Sasha said in a conspiratorial whisper.

"Small favors," Mitchell whispered back.

Two more couples got in and the driver took off. It wasn't long before Sasha grew comfortable with the bumpy on-the-wrong-side-of-the-road driving. She was no longer mortified sitting next to Mitchell. She enjoyed it each time their hips bumped or his arm rested against hers when the driver made his two-wheel turns, or when he reached over without a word and enveloped her hand in his. Nope, she didn't mind the ride at all.

The drive took about twenty minutes. By the time they pulled up to the bay, there was already a line of brightly dressed partygoers ready to board. They could hear the beat of music coming from the ship.

"Have you ever been on a party cruise ship?" Mitchell asked as they inched their way up on line.

"This will be a first."

"Then I'm glad you'll have your first experience with me."

The double entendre wasn't lost on either of them as their gazes connected and sparkled against the lights strung across the hulking ship.

Mitchell helped her up the gangway and they were immediately swept up in the full-blown party on board. Music pumped, bodies swayed, and drinks freely flowed.

"What can I get you?" Mitchell asked, playing the perfect host.

"Hmmm, I'd love a drink. Rum punch?"

"An island specialty," he quipped. "Come with me. Food and beverages are below."

He led her down a short flight of stairs, they wound their way around the jumping, bumping bodies and down a narrow walkway to the bar that was packed two deep.

Mitchell squeezed his way in between several guests until he was at the counter.

"I'll have two rum punches," he said. The bartender handed him his drinks and Mitchell held them over his head as he found his way back to Sasha.

"Here ya go," he said, handing Sasha her drink. Some of the sweet frosty liquor dripped over the side of the glass and onto Sasha's fingers. What Mitchell did next had Sasha's knees quivering beneath her—he took her sticky fingers and one by one inserted them into his mouth, sucking off the sweet juice.

Her heart pounded against her chest. Sasha was afraid to look into Mitchell's eyes and when she did her breath shimmied in her throat. Something dark and dangerous hovering in his gaze reached out for her, stroked her. She could barely think when he released the last finger from his mouth.

"Taste it," he said. "I think you'll really like it."

Sasha swallowed. She ran her tongue across her suddenly dry lips before slowly lifting the glass to her mouth. She took a long, slow sip.

Mitchell couldn't take his eyes off her, and Sasha felt as if he were stripping her naked in front of all of these people in the middle of the ocean. And she didn't want him to stop him.

It had been so long since she'd felt desirable, felt like the kind of woman a man like Mitchell Davenport would want. But that's how she felt tonight, turned on and reckless. She wanted to show him just how much. This was going to be a long night.

After the erotic display at the bar Mitchell didn't let Sasha out of his sight for the rest of the evening. Wherever she turned he was there, getting her whatever she needed, listening to her, laughing with her, holding her. They danced under the moonlight, fast, slow and something in between. Their bodies seemed to be made for each other, fitting together perfectly like pieces to a puzzle. As the boat took them farther away from the shore, Mitchell pointed out the beautiful mountain landscape of Antigua.

"See that mountain over there?" he said, pointing to the northeast. Sasha's gaze followed his outstretched arm.

"Yes."

"The prime minister of Antigua renamed that mountain Mount Obama after our president."

"That is so incredible," Sasha said. "I'm still amazed that the United States has its first African-American president. There were times when I didn't believe it was going to happen."

"Neither did I, and he definitely has his hands full." Mitchell slid his arm around Sasha's waist. "But tonight is not a night for discussing politics."

Sasha turned in his arms and gazed up at him. Her voice dropped to a soft, husky whisper. "Then what kind of night is it?"

"A night for finding out about each other."

"In what way?" she asked as they moved to the beat of a reggae love song.

"In whatever way will satisfy the questions that we want answered," he breathed in her ear as he held her close against his hard body.

Ohmygoodness.

The music came to an abrupt end, and Mitchell took Sasha's hand and led her over to the railing.

The ship swayed ever so slightly against the gently rolling waves. The motion was soothing, like a lullaby, and gave him the perfect opportunity to bump up against Sasha without having to make excuses.

"The night is just as you said it would be," Sasha said. "Actually it's better."

Mitchell turned to look at her. He leaned his hip against the rail and stretched out his hand to brush her hair away from the sides of her face. "Do you have any idea how beautiful you are?"

Sasha started to speak, but didn't know what to say. How long had it been since someone called her beautiful?

"I don't want you to think that all of this is just some big come-on." Mitchell straightened up, gazed out onto the ocean. "It's not." His long fingers gripped the railing.

Sasha watched his profile, saw the struggle that danced along the strong line of his jaw. Her slender fingers covered his. "I know this is not a game for me," she admitted softly. "But I must admit, this is my first time…I mean, my first time meeting a strange man and feeling the way that I do about you."

Mitchell suddenly turned toward her. "How *do* you feel?"

Sasha's throat worked up and down as she tried to find the words to explain what had been going on in her heart and her mind from the moment she'd met Mitchell Davenport.

"All I know for sure is that this is something new, something I've never experienced before, and until I find out everything that I can find out about you and what's going on inside my head—I don't want it to end." She paused a moment, stunned by her own admission. The one consolation was the motto that April always lived by, *If you put your cards on the table, you'll find out in no time just what everybody else has in their hand.* Well, she'd definitely put her cards on the table. Now it was just a matter of seeing what cards Mitchell had in his hand.

Under the light of the moon, Sasha watched, transfixed, as he came closer, his eyes boring into hers. Everything seemed to be happening in slow motion. She watched it all as if standing outside of her body. He lowered his head. His hands slid behind her neck, pulling her gently toward him. Sasha held her breath. She raised up on her toes to meet his waiting lips. And when they touched hers, a million lights exploded in her brain. His deep groan mixed with her heavy sigh and drifted off on the ocean breeze. His tongue grazed her lips and she tasted the sweetness of the rum punch. Sasha gave in to the tenderness of his kiss awakening her body to an entirely new level of sensation.

His tongue played, teased and taunted her, causing shivers to run up and down her spine. He held her close, allowing Sasha to feel just how desperately he wanted her.

The kiss lasted only for an instant, but it felt like an eternity in heaven to Sasha as she relived it over and over in her mind throughout the rest of the evening.

By the time the ship docked more than an hour later, Sasha and Mitchell were ready to really get started with their night.

On the drive back in the van, they both pretended that their thoughts weren't headed in the same direction. They talked about the food. They talked about the drinks. They talked about how beautiful all of the people on the ship looked. What they didn't talk about was what was going on inside of each of them—the growing need that could no longer be contained by small talk and polite conversation. What they wanted more than anything else was to find a way to put out the fire, to discover if what they imagined could be anything close to the real thing.

Sasha's heart thumped dangerously loud as they walked along the path toward their rooms. It took all of her concentration to put one foot in front of the other and keep her body from shaking.

"Nightcap?" Mitchell asked as they drew closer to the beachfront bar.

What she needed was to be clearheaded. The last thing she wanted was to blame whatever happened the rest of the night on one drink too many. She already felt slightly light-headed from several glasses of rum punch.

"No thanks. I think I've had my fill for the evening."

They continued down the manicured pathway toward the corridor of rooms that brought to mind old-world Spain, with the whitewashed stone fronts and open-air stairways leading to the upper levels.

They approached Mitchell's door first. Sasha felt her knees wobble. He walked right past it as if he didn't see it and stopped in front of her door. He turned to look down into her eyes that were lit with quiet longing, questions and anticipation.

She clasped her hands in front of her, then, suddenly flustered and uncertain, she unclasped them and opened her purse to retrieve her key. *Guess the night ends here,* she thought, pulling the key from her bag.

"Sasha…"

He said her name so softly she wasn't sure whether she'd imagined it or if it was real. She glanced up.

"Yes?" She heard her own voice tremble and wondered if Mitchell heard that as well.

"I guess this is what they call an awkward end to

a first date," Mitchell said. He shifted his weight from one foot to the other, slung his hands in his pockets then looked at Sasha. "I was hoping that maybe you could stop by my room for a little while."

"Oh," she sputtered. "I…I…sure."

"Great."

If Sasha didn't know better she'd swear that she saw Mitchell breathe a sigh of relief as he turned toward his door. He put the key in the lock, turned the knob and pushed the door open, then stepped aside to let Sasha pass. The moment she stepped into the room she couldn't remember the advice that April had given her—was she supposed to go to his place or was he supposed to come to hers? At this point it didn't matter. The time had come.

Chapter 7

Mitchell flipped on the light as Sasha stepped into the room. She was pleasantly surprised to see that his room was as neat as hers, and she wondered if he'd gotten some advice from a friend of his as well.

"I can order something from room service if you're hungry or thirsty," Mitchell said. He shrugged out of his jacket and hung it on the back of the chair.

"Water is fine. I'm really full after all the food we ate on the ship," she said, stifling a laugh.

Mitchell chuckled in response. "That's true. One thing about going on vacation, you always eat more than you ever possibly could when you're back at home. I found that out the hard way last time I went away."

Sasha strolled farther into the room, walking toward the terrace doors. She slid them open and stepped outside and leaned against the balcony. Mitchell stepped out behind her.

"It really is quite beautiful here," Sasha said softly, looking out toward the horizon.

Mitchell moved close to her. There was barely any space separating them. He looked down into her upturned face. "Everything from the flowers to the mountains to the ocean, the sandy beaches— nothing can compare to how beautiful you are, Sasha," he said. "And I'm not just saying all those things because I want to make love to you," he admitted.

Sasha could not believe what she'd just heard. He'd actually said he wanted to make love to her. She reached up and stroked his jaw. "Do you really mean that, or is it just a line that you give all of the single island ladies?" There was a hint of mischief in her voice, but her question was sincere.

"I have no reason to lie to you. If there was someone else I wanted to be with, I probably could've done that a long time ago. It's not what I wanted. I know as well as you do that something sparked between us from the moment we laid eyes on each other. If I'm wrong, tell me and I'll leave it alone. Right now. I'll never bring it up again."

Sasha knew what he was trying to say without actually coming out and saying the words. He wanted her to admit that she wanted him just as much as he wanted her. "You're right," she said. "I've never felt this way about someone so quickly." She lowered her head for a moment trying to gather her thoughts. She looked up into his questioning eyes. "I feel the same way you do. I've wanted you from the moment I saw you, from the moment we started talking, from the moment… you kissed me for the first time." She listened to her confession pour from her lips. She did believe the things that she was saying. What was even more distressing was she could not believe what she was feeling. Was it possible to actually feel this deeply this quickly about someone she barely knew? Would she wake up tomorrow and regret the decision she was about to make? Or would this be the greatest thing that had ever happened to her?

Mitchell watched the varied emotions flit across Sasha's face. It was almost as if he were watching his own reflection. He felt the same way, certain and uncertain, yet knowing that there was no turning back, and he didn't want to. He threaded his long fingers behind her neck, pulling her closer to him. He lowered his head. His eyes focused on her lips as they slightly parted, waiting for him to touch them, make them his own. He felt her intake of breath as his lips met hers, soft, sweet, delectable like the succulent fruits of the Caribbean island.

He took her mouth, slow and easy like the sultry beat of the ocean waves against the shore. He felt his body react to the softness of hers as he pulled her closer.

She stepped up to him, pressing her body flush against his own. Every dip, every curve fit perfectly. Sasha moaned against his mouth, which only inflamed the desire that he felt for her.

She felt his body harden, stiffen, his heat pressing between her warm thighs.

His large hands slid down the curve of her spine, cupping her behind, pulling her closer, locking her against him. He groaned as Sasha lifted her fingers and played with the shell of his ear.

"Sasha," Mitchell moaned against her mouth. "The whole world can see us standing on the balcony." He stroked her hair, ran his finger along the curve of her jaw.

Sasha looked up at him, feeling bold. "I don't care," she said. "Let them look."

Mitchell tossed his head back and laughed. "You never cease to amaze me." He took her hand and stepped back into the room, shutting the terrace doors behind them. He drew the drapes. "There are some things that I plan to do to you tonight that I don't want anybody to witness, other than you and I."

Sasha languidly ran her tongue across her lips. She shrugged off her jacket and dropped it on the corner of the bed then leaned down and released the straps of her sandals and stepped out of them.

Mitchell crossed the room, turned off the overhead lights and turned on the softer lights on the nightstands next to the bed. He extended his hand to her. She took it, and he drew her close.

"Are you sure this is what you want to do?" Mitchell asked a final time.

Sasha nodded, uncertain of what she would say if she tried to speak.

They could hear the sound of partygoers outside the door. Laughter rippled up and down the corridor, drawing their attention and for a moment breaking the spell between them. The noise gradually quieted down, and Sasha and Mitchell returned their attention to each other. He reached behind her and unzipped her dress. She gasped softly, his eyes questioned her, and her response was an unequivocal yes.

Sasha worked the buttons of Mitchell's starched white shirt until it was completely undone and fell away from the hard lines of his muscular chest.

She ran the tips of her nails across the rippled muscles of his six-pack. He drew in a short breath, then eased Sasha's dress over the curves of her body until it slipped away and pooled at her feet.

"Oh…my…God," Mitchell uttered when his gaze fell upon the curves, the softness, the sensuous delight that was Sasha's banging body. He lowered his head and sought her lips.

Sasha's eyes drifted closed as she stretched her arms upward and linked her fingers behind the curve of Mitchell's neck.

His gentle fingers played with her spine, causing shivers to run up and down her body. The hard bulge in his crotch pressed roughly against her, and she felt her own desire rise and flow between her thighs.

A quick pop by nimble fingers released her strapless bra. Mitchell pulled it away and tossed it on the floor. He took a step back to take her in— and it was a feast.

Her breasts were full, lush and perfect. Her nipples hard and pointed, ready to be tasted, and he did.

Sasha let out a gasp of delight when Mitchell's hot lips covered her right nipple, gently tugging, laving and sucking on it, making her legs tremble in response. He massaged the other, running his thumb across the hardened peak. Any doubt or misgiving vanished, replaced with a need so demanding that she was certain if she didn't have him, and soon, she would explode. She wanted to be sure that the explosion happened with Mitchell buried deep inside her. She released his belt and zipper. His slacks dropped to his ankles, and he kicked them out of the way.

She reached down, slid her hand beneath the band of his shorts and tenderly stroked the length of him, stunned by the silky texture that covered what felt like steel.

Mitchell shuddered. The muscles in his neck tightened like knotted rope. Something deep and dark rumbled in his throat. In a smooth move he reversed their positions until Sasha's back was to the bed. He eased her down.

She lifted her legs onto the bed and slid over to give him room to join her.

For a moment, he stood above her, drinking her in like a man starved for nourishment, before pushing his shorts down over his hips and stepping out of them. Sasha drew in a breath of awe and alarm. Even in the dim light, he looked lethal. She trembled.

Mitchell moved toward her, stretching the length of his body alongside hers. He caressed her face as she turned her head to kiss the inside of his palm.

His hand drifted down, trailing across the rise of her breasts to the hollow of her stomach to the hot darkness nestled between her legs. She jumped ever so slightly when he began patting her there, gently, in a teasing rhythm that soon had her writhing and moaning softly. He pushed away the barely-there string of her thong to find her wet and ready.

Instinctively her hips rose as his finger played with the throbbing bud, then slid farther up into the slick wetness of her opening.

Sasha gripped the sheets as her body took on a will of its own, moving up and down against the steady stroke of his fingers.

His rhythm built in intensity. Her head spun as an unbearable heat filled her.

"That's it," he cooed, urging her on. "You feel so good," he murmured. He lowered his head and took her breast into his mouth as he continued to finger her.

"Oooh, God," she cried as the first spasm was unleashed and roared through her in a wave that curled her toes and separated her from reality. Her breasts rose and fell as her orgasm slowly subsided, leaving her weak yet wanting even more.

Slowly she opened her eyes and stared into his.

"Ready for me now?" he asked, slowly easing his fingers out.

She whimpered, suddenly feeling empty. Numbly she nodded her head, then reality hit. "Wait," she managed to say. Pulling herself up on her hands and knees, she crawled to the edge of the bed and felt on the floor for her purse. She took out two condoms then returned to her spot next to Mitchell.

"Why don't you do the honors?" he said.

With shaky fingers she tore the packet open and removed the thin sheath. Nervously eyeing him she placed the condom on his swollen tip and rolled it down his length.

Mitchell bit down on his bottom lip to keep from groaning out loud. The heat of her hands, the way she subtly jerked him up and down while putting on the condom was nearly his undoing.

He gripped her wrist. "Okay, okay…you gotta stop," he said.

Amusement sparkled in her eyes and a sense of power flooded through her at the thought that she could make him feel anywhere near as awesome as he'd made her feel moments ago.

"What would you have me do instead?" she taunted.

"Lie back and open your legs for me. Let me in."

Locking her gaze with his, she did as he asked. He reached around her and snatched a pillow from the head of the bed. "Lift up," he ordered, and slid the pillow beneath her hips.

He moved into a position above her, snug between her parted thighs. He cupped his hands underneath her knees and rose up on his own. He pushed her thighs back toward her chest until they were wide, stretched out on either side of his shoulders.

He didn't need a hand to guide him. Like radar he found her opening. That first contact was electric and shot through both of them. He pressed. The tip breached her opening and she gasped, feeling her insides begin to spread as he slowly pushed into her.

Mitchell lowered his head and kissed her, filling her mouth with his hungry tongue, muffling her moans as he began to move deep within her.

The nothings that he whispered in her ear were anything but sweet. They were hot, erotic, downright freaky. And she gave just as good as she got.

"Like this…" she said, thrusting her hips hard against him, causing his eyes to slam shut and an expletive to gush from his mouth.

He opened his eyes and looked down at her, his gaze intense and fierce. "No. More like this," he ground out, cupping her firm behind in his palms and lifting her lower body up and down like she weighed no more than a loaf of bread.

Her head spun. Her fingers dug into his shoulder blades when he hit a spot that had never before been reached. She screamed when he tapped the spot again, and again, winding his hips, pulling almost all the way out then plunging back in again.

Sasha couldn't catch her breath as the sensuous

assault continued and escalated until her entire body was consumed by heat, and tremors shot from the balls of her feet, down the backs of her legs that were pointed toward the ceiling, and exploded in the center of her being.

The sound that erupted from the core of her soul spiraled into the heated air, unfamiliar, raw and ragged, as Mitchell moved harder and faster, drawing closer to his own desperately needed climax.

Sasha managed to slide her hand down between their thrusting bodies to cup and massage him, while using her internal muscles to squeeze and release his cock, pumping out every drop of his essence.

"Ugg!" He slammed into her one final time, pushing himself to the hilt, his body stiff and jerky as if electrified, before collapsing on top of her.

Their heavy breathing and the thumping beats of their hearts were the only sounds in the room.

Sasha lay beneath Mitchell, listening to his heart pound against her chest, mesmerized by what had just transpired. There had not been many men in her life. She could count the ones she'd slept with on one hand with fingers left over. But this…this thing that had happened between her and Mitchell was beyond carnal lust. It was a reckoning. The way he'd made her feel was how they wrote sex scenes in romance novels. Surreal. Impossible. But she'd experienced it. She could testify.

As his erection began to soften it sent another shudder rippling through Sasha, stunning her with the realization that she had anything left. She moaned in need.

Totally in tune to her body's reaction, Mitchell slowly pulled out, ensuring that the condom was still intact before bringing Sasha to another spine-curling orgasm with his fingers.

Spent and weak, they curled their bodies against each other and drifted off to sleep, only to wake a short time later to begin all over again.

They made love throughout the night, taking short breaks to talk, to laugh at what they were doing and to replenish their bodies with much-needed water.

Just before daybreak, Sasha coaxed Mitchell out onto the terrace and beneath the splash of stars and the waning moonlight, with only the ocean as their audience, she leaned over the railing and let him take her.

Chapter 8

Mitchell couldn't remember the last time he'd slept so hard and so well. He stretched and groaned as sleep began to slip away even as he wanted to burrow down in the sweet dream of making love to Sasha Carrington.

Something nudged him. It wasn't a dream. He opened his eyes, sat up. He felt the opposite side of the bed. Empty. "Sasha!" He threw his legs over the side of the bed and stood. "Sasha..." Rubbing his eyes free of sleep he looked around the room and knew something was wrong. All of her things were gone.

He shook his head. Had he imagined it all? He

glanced down at his half-mast, and it jerked, as if answering his question, and he knew that there was no way it was a dream. He turned back toward the bed, tossing the sheets, looking for a note. There wasn't one on either nightstand, on the television or tacked to the door.

He ran his hand across the top of his head and yawned loudly. Why would she leave like that? Without a word? Did he say or do something in his sleep? He wandered into the bathroom. After he got himself together he'd give her a call. He turned on the shower full-blast and stepped under the pulsing hot water.

Dressed and refreshed, he sat on the side of the bed and pulled the phone toward him. He looked at the phone instructions for dialing room-to-room and placed a call to Sasha. Frowning, he listened to the phone ring and ring. *Maybe she's gone over to the buffet to grab some food,* he thought, hanging up.

He grabbed his key and cell phone from the table and headed out, determined to shake off the bad feeling that was brewing inside him.

When he stepped out of his room he was momentarily cut off by one of the staff assisting a couple with their luggage. They exchanged brief pleasantries and Mitchell was about to walk away when he realized that the couple and the hotel help had stopped in front of Sasha's door.

"Hey, whadda you doing?" he demanded when the staffer stuck a key in Sasha's door.

The trio turned to stare at him in confusion.

"Is there a problem?" the husband asked, putting his arm protectively around his wife's waist.

The staffer turned the key and pushed the door open. Mitchell quickly stepped around the couple and peeked inside. Empty. Totally, save for the furniture.

"Do you mind?" the wife said.

"Look, buddy, I don't know what your problem is. This is our room."

"I'm sorry." Mitchell backed away. He didn't know what to make of what he'd just seen. Where could she have gone? Confused, he walked down the corridor and across the walkway toward the reception area.

At the front desk, the concierge said, "Good morning, sir, how can I help you?"

"I'm looking for Sasha Carrington. She was in the room right next to mine, but I just saw a couple moving into her room. Is she somewhere else on the resort?" He suddenly felt like an idiot.

"Let me take a look." The receptionist went to the computer, and, after several keystrokes, she looked up at Mitchell. "I'm sorry, Ms. Carrington checked out earlier this morning."

"Checked out?"

"Yes, she left about nine o'clock this morning."

"I don't understand."

"I'm sorry, sir. Is there something else I can help you with?"

Mitchell stood for several moments, uncertain of what to do next. This just didn't make any sense. Out of the blue she picks up and leaves?

"Sir?"

Mitchell blinked. "I'm…no. Thank you." He turned and walked away, heading back toward his room. Halfway there, he stopped and changed his mind, turned around and headed back in the opposite direction. If she was gone, so be it. He was here to take care of business and have a good time while he was at it. And that's exactly what he intended to do. He should've known better than to get involved with someone, especially someone like Sasha Carrington.

Sasha watched the landscape unfold in front of her as the van bumped and chugged along the ruddy dirt roads. She knew she should have left Mitchell a note. She should've had the decency to say something to him. Instead she'd sneaked away like a thief in the night. It was better this way, she decided. No ties, no strings, no explanations. At some point, she would've had to try to get away from him anyway. They were expecting her at the hotel. But that didn't stop her from feeling guilty. The night she'd spent with Mitchell was unlike any other that she'd spent with a man before. She could still smell him on her skin. She could still feel his hands on her body. Simply thinking of the magic he'd worked on her body made her eyes roll into the back of her head. Those were sensations and images she would never forget, no matter how far away she was from him.

When she'd tiptoed out of his room shortly before dawn, she'd hesitated. She wanted to tell him everything—the reason why she was really in Antigua. Of course, she couldn't. It would be a violation of her contract and that was a risk she was not willing to take. So, rather than lie, she decided to do the easy thing and slip away.

Well, if her decision was so perfect then why did she feel so awful?

She held her cell phone in her hand, debating whether to call him. It was a debate she'd had with herself for the past few hours. The answer was always the same. *No.*

When she'd returned to her room that morning, the first thing that she did was call April. They'd talked for nearly an hour, with Sasha pouring out everything that had happened and her feelings about the way she'd handled things. April assured her that she was doing the right thing. As difficult as it was, it would get easier, April reassured her.

"You went down there for one reason and one reason alone," April had said. "That was to enter the competition and win. Anything else is just extra. Hold on to the wonderful memories, and if it's meant to be, you two will run into each other again."

Sasha held on to that thought as the van pulled closer to her destination. *If it's meant to be we'll see each other again,* she thought.

The island came alive as the people of Antigua began moving around the rural streets. Sasha was once again saddened by the stark difference between the tourist areas and where the people of Antigua actually lived.

Many of the houses that she passed along the road were no more than shacks, and animals wandered freely, often blocking traffic on the narrow streets. Barefoot children played outside on the worn steps of the ramshackle houses and in the yards that barely had any grass. The gulf between poverty and wealth was painfully visible. She supposed it was like this in every part of the world—the haves and the have-nots. Some places just hid the poverty better than others. What was most amazing for Sasha was that everybody in Antigua seemed happy. She guessed that if you were going to be poor, the best place to be was on an island like Antigua, where you could let your troubles float away and you could fill your belly with fruit plucked from trees.

The lush landscape opened up in front of her, and the small one-room shacks began to disappear. In the distance, she spotted the rising mountaintops and the mansions tucked away in the hillside. The view was magnificent. And she suddenly wished that Mitchell was here to share it with her. She gripped her cell phone. *One call,* she thought. *Just to explain.* But then April's warning voice rang in her head. *Leave it alone.*

What she needed to concentrate on was what lay in front of her, not what she'd left behind.

Sasha leaned back against the rough leather seat cushion and closed her eyes. Within moments, visions of Mitchell loomed behind her lids. The sound of his voice echoed in her ears. Images of his magnificent naked body played havoc with her libido. She squirmed in her seat. *This can't go on,* she thought, hoping that with all the activity ahead of her, memories of Mitchell would soon fade away. Yet, there was a part of her that knew that was not to be.

The van began to slow. Sasha opened her eyes.

In front of her was the new hotel that she would be living in for the duration of her stay in Antigua. Her heart pounded. This was it, the reason she'd come. The van came to a rumbling halt.

"Here we are," the driver called out. He hopped out of the van and came around to the side to open Sasha's door. He helped her down the two steps and took her luggage from the back of the van and walked with her to the front door of the hotel. Sasha reached into her purse and took out the local currency. She handed him what she thought was a five-dollar bill, hoping it was enough.

"Thank you very much," she said.

"Enjoy your stay, miss." The driver pocketed the money and hurried back to the van.

A doorman in a bright-white jacket, came out to greet her. "Good morning, miss. Welcome to Season." He reached for her bags and led her to the entrance. As Sasha followed, her pulse quickened. This was it, she thought.

The doorman set her bags down at the reception desk. Sasha walked up to the counter.

"Good morning. How may I help you?"

"Sasha Carrington. I should have a reservation. I'm one of the *Heartbreak Hotel* contestants." She felt a little silly saying that until she saw the receptionist's expression.

The young woman's face brightened. Her eyes

widened in delight. "Welcome! Your room is ready for you." She input some information into the computer, printed out a sheet of paper and handed it to Sasha. "Here's all the information you'll need for your stay." She took several brochures from the rack in front of her and passed them to Sasha. "These will tell you about all the activities, where everything is located and all of the amenities that are available to you here at the hotel during your stay."

Sasha took the brochures and tucked them into her purse. "Thanks."

The receptionist handed Sasha as plastic card. "Here's your key." She then rang a bell on her desk and a bellhop appeared. "Ms. Carrington is on the third floor, John. Would you please take her to her room?"

"Certainly. Follow me miss." The bellhop took Sasha's suitcases and walked toward the bank of elevators. "First time in Antigua?"

"Yes, it is."

"Everyone who comes here always comes back."

"Is that right?" Sasha gave a half smile.

"I can guarantee we will see you again," he said with conviction.

The elevator doors slid open, and they stepped inside. "Are you one of the contestants for the reality television show?" he asked her.

"Yes I am. Have many of the others arrived yet?"

"I know that the camera crew is here. Some of the contestants have arrived as well. They're all on the third floor."

"Is this where they're going to be filming?" she asked.

John chuckled from deep in his belly. "Oh no, miss. From what I hear most of the filming will be done at a hotel just up the road." The elevator doors slid open. "And from what I've seen, you all have your work cut out for you." He chuckled again.

They walked down the carpeted corridor until they reached Sasha's room. John turned to her and held out his hand. "Your card, miss."

Sasha handed him her key card, and he swung the door open and stepped aside to let her pass. He set down her bags in the center of the room.

"You can adjust the temperature," he advised. He drew back the drapes. "You have a fantastic view of the beach." He turned to face her and put her key card on the dresser. "Is there anything I can get you before I leave?"

"No. Thank you very much. You've been extremely helpful." She opened her purse, took out another five dollars and handed it to the bellhop.

He pocketed the money, nodded and headed for the door.

"Umm, before you leave…you said we have a lot of work cut out for us. What did you mean by that?"

"The hotel where they'll be filming…it hasn't been used for almost ten years. I guess that will give you an idea of how hard your job will be." He smiled. "Good luck." He closed the door quietly behind him.

Sasha crossed the room and walked to the terrace. She opened the glass doors and stepped onto the small balcony. *Ten years!* She couldn't begin to imagine what kind of shape the hotel would be in or what they would have them do when all of the contestants arrived.

She breathed in deeply. The scent of the ocean and the aroma of grilled food wafted in the air, cooled by the ocean breeze. This time yesterday she was preparing for her date with Mitchell. *What a difference a day makes.* Still, she couldn't get over the nagging feeling that she should have at least left him a note. But how was she going to explain her disappearance for the next two weeks? He'd made it clear that he wanted to spend much of his trip with her. That was not possible. At least not under the circumstances.

She turned away from the beauty of the blue-and-white landscape and walked back into the room to check out her new space.

All this cloak-and-dagger business was so unlike her, she mused, as she opened the closet door, happy to see a fluffy terry-cloth robe hanging on the hook. She shut the door and went to peek in the bathroom.

What was more unlike her, however, was sleeping with a man she'd only met days earlier. She got a shiver at the thought of it.

She opened the shower door, flushed the toilet and turned on the faucets to make sure everything worked.

The spell of the Caribbean certainly did strange things to people—well at least to her, and maybe to Mitchell, too, she decided, turning everything off. But what if she ran into him again? How could she ever look him in the eye?

She shook her head to dispel the thoughts that clouded her mind with questions she couldn't answer. "Move on," she said out loud, stepping out of the bathroom. In the next few days her life was destined to turn in a completely new direction, and she needed to be focused.

Determined to keep thoughts of Mitchell and their night together out of her head, she went about the business of unpacking. Then she was going for a swim.

Sasha tossed her cell phone, tanning lotion, an extra towel and her key card into her beach bag and headed out. She'd pulled her hair into a loose knot on top of her head and had selected a burnt-orange-and-gold one-piece suit. She tied a gauzy see-through wrap in orange, gold and bright blue around her waist, stuck her feet in her flip-flops and headed out.

When she entered the corridor, a door opened on the opposite side and a young woman, maybe around thirty, stepped out, apparently en route to the beach as well. She had a fierce short haircut that Sasha had always wished she could wear but knew she didn't have the face for. She was compact, maybe about five-five, and curvy, much like April. She spotted Sasha.

"Hi, heading to the beach or the pool?" she asked with a big smile. She tossed a multicolored towel over her shoulder.

"Beach. How about you?"

They began walking toward the elevator.

"Me too. I love the challenge of the waves. Misty," she said.

Sasha didn't catch it at first then realized it was her name and not a weather forecast. "Oh, I'm Sasha. Sasha Carrington."

Misty bobbed her head in approval. "Carrington. Cool last name. Mine is Smith and I've always had the feeling that no one ever believes me. Misty Smith, sounds like an alias, right?" She turned to Sasha for confirmation.

Sasha couldn't help but laugh. "You may have a point," she managed over her giggles.

Misty chuckled as well. "I've gotten used to it."

They stopped in front of the elevator and Misty pressed the down button. "So I'm guessing if you're here on the third floor you must either be part of the television crew or one of the contestants."

The door opened.

"One of the contestants," Sasha said.

"Me, too." Misty beamed. "Isn't it great? I mean it's a chance of a lifetime. The winner gets to run their own hotel!" She arched her head back and closed her eyes in what looked like ecstasy. She pulled herself together. "You have to excuse me. I've never won a damned thing in my life, so this is more than I can handle without doing the happy dance every five minutes."

"I know what you mean. I can't believe I'm at a resort in Antigua and everything is free!"

They cracked up laughing as the elevator descended.

"Is every hotel in Antigua on the beach?" Sasha asked as they secured a spot and spread their blankets.

"Seems like it. I read that there are over three hundred beaches in Antigua. Is this your first time here?"

"Yep. What about you?"

"Yep. I'm a virgin, too. I've been to Barbados

and Jamaica but never here. Where are you from?" she asked, rubbing sunscreen on her arms and legs.

"Savannah, Georgia. And you?"

"The big bad apple. New York."

"I have family there. Crazy place," Sasha said taking off her sandals.

"That it is, but I'd never live anywhere else." Misty popped up. "I'm heading in."

Sasha followed suit and they jogged to the shore, waded out then dove in.

They swam for at least a half hour before dragging themselves back to their spot on the beach and collapsing on their towels.

"Whew. I haven't done that in ages," Misty said, breathing heavily. "Not since the last time I was on vacation."

"I love to swim," Sasha said, propped up on her elbows as she held her face toward the warm sun. "Takes the stress out."

"I belong to the YWCA back home, but I rarely have a chance to use the pool."

"What do you do for a living?"

"I'm a chef at a health food restaurant in SoHo." She shrugged her right shoulder. "It's pretty cool, but I'm tired of working for other people. I'd love to have a place of my own, put my stamp on it. Know what I mean?" She turned to look at Sasha. "But I guess you would, too, or you wouldn't be here."

The sharp reality that they would be competitors for the same prize suddenly struck them.

"Doesn't mean we can't be friends," Sasha said, voicing what they were both feeling.

Misty smiled. "True. You can never have too many of those. Anyhow, who's to say we won't be on the same team and need each other's help and expertise."

"Exactly!"

They both knew there could only be one winner, but it never hurt to have an ally no matter how the competition went.

As they talked about their lives and aspirations, things they liked, the latest celebrity scandals and having Obama in the White House, Sasha thought that April would really like meeting Misty. She knew the three of them would have a blast together.

Mitchell sat at the bar nursing a very strong rum punch. The beats of reggae, calypso, R & B and even some hip-hop brought people to the small dance floor sheltered by overhead netting in an attempt to keep the bugs out.

Laughter bubbled all around him; hearty conversations and soft whisperings for late-night plans bounced from table to table.

What an idiot he had been, he chastised himself. He'd had the chance to walk away and stay away from Sasha at the airport, but he wouldn't listen to his own good sense.

The truth of it all was that he was in no emotional shape to deal with anyone on an even playing field. His emotions constantly vacillated from outright anger at women in general to distrust and then to an overwhelming desire to be back in a relationship. If he was ever going to get his head right he was going to have to find a middle ground. What he needed was some time on his own to figure things out, lick his wounds and get on with his life. He wasn't being fair to himself or to Sasha to get involved.

It was just as well that she'd picked up and left. He tossed down the rest of his drink and asked for another. Nothing could have come of it anyway. He had absolutely nothing to offer a woman— except great sex. That was one thing he knew he was good at.

That realization ignited his still-raw feelings of worthlessness. Maybe he should just be put out to stud and call it a day, he thought morosely.

It was probably all that Sasha had wanted anyway. Some good sex, a little conversation and move on.

They were both adults. No strings. No commitments. He took a swallow of his drink.

"Is anyone sitting here?"

Mitchell turned toward the sound of the voice. *Hmmmm.* "No. Be my guest."

"Thanks." A woman hopped up on the stool.

The soft scent of her perfume floated to him. He took her in from the corner of his eye. Golden-brown from the sun. Long and slender... athletic. Small breasts. Great legs. Short, curly hair. Cute face.

"What are you drinking?" he asked.

"Hmmm, undecided." She peeked at his glass then pointed at it with her finger. "Is that good?"

"Yeah. It's become my favorite. Rum punch. Pretty strong though," he warned.

She smiled and he noticed the slight gap in her front teeth which gave her a little-girl look. "I think I'll try it. You'll make sure no one takes advantage of me," she said, her voice suddenly low and teasing.

Mitchell ran his gaze quickly over her. "Of course I will." He signaled for the bartender. "A rum punch for the lady." He turned to her. "Since we're going to be sharing happy hour together, my name is Mitchell Davenport."

"Joy Martin."

"Pleasure, Joy."

The bartender returned with Joy's drink. Mitchell raised his glass and she touched hers to his.

"To new friends," he said.

She grinned, flashing a gap-toothed smile. "To

new friends that become old ones." She winked. "So, Mitchell Davenport," she began, turning on her stool so that she faced him, "why don't you tell me all about yourself? We have the whole night…"

Chapter 9

After the vigorous swim in the ocean then chatting on the beach until the sun disappeared beyond the horizon, Sasha and Misty headed back to their rooms.

"Have you met any of the other contestants?" Sasha asked as they crossed the walkway leading to the front of the hotel.

"No, I've met a few of the crew members, though. According to the letter, we could arrive as early as the day before yesterday but no later than Friday, so I guess some folks are still on their way. I know I wanted to come early and get the lay of the land and some R and R before the real work began."

"Me, too." Sasha didn't bother to tell Misty that her mini vacation had begun on Jolly Beach, or that she'd met the greatest man while she was there and had subsequently walked out on him because legally she couldn't tell him where she was going or the real reason why she was in Antigua in the first place. "Did you find it hard not to tell people the truth about being here?"

Misty frowned for a moment. "Not really. My family back home knows. And since I came straight here, the only people I've really interacted with since I arrived are the hotel help and you." She paused a moment. "Why?"

"Hmmm, nothing. Just asking." Sasha hesitated a moment, debating about posing her hypothetical question. "Misty…"

"Yeah." She ran a towel over her hair.

"Say you met someone while you were here and you really hit it off, but you couldn't tell them why you were here, so you lie. You can't tell them why you can't see them anymore, so you disappear."

"Sounds like a *CSI* episode," she joked. "What's the question?"

"Would you do something like that if saying anything meant that the biggest opportunity of your life would be snatched away from you?"

Misty twisted her lips in concentration. "How well do I know this person?"

"Not very. You sorta just met."

Misty waved her hand in dismissal. "Just met! Ha, I wouldn't even sweat it. Guys do it all the time."

They pushed through the glass doors and into the cool interior of the hotel.

"I'm going to take a nap," Misty said, yawning. "If you want to hook up for dinner, knock on my door. If not, I'll order room service."

"Okay."

They stepped on the elevator and rode up to the third floor.

"If I don't hear a knock by nine, I'll order in," Misty said, yawning again as she inserted her key card in the slot.

"Rest well. I'm feeling pretty tired myself." Sasha stepped inside her room and locked the door behind her. Before she could even think of taking a nap she needed to shower, then she'd give her mom a call and check in on Tristan. She was still amazed that, having left her husband, she hadn't been bombarded with calls from home. Under normal circumstances that would have been worth at least a dozen calls a day. Everyone seemed to be doing quite well without her, she thought.

Mitchell was probably doing fine without her too. She stepped into the shower and turned her face up to the water. Did it matter to him that she was gone? Had he asked about her? Did he think that something had happened, that she'd been kidnapped? Or just that she was a swinging single woman on vacation looking for a good time?

What difference did it make? They'd had their time together—end of story. In a few days, she was going to begin the journey of her life, and she hoped that the other contestants wouldn't be too upset when *she* went home with the big prize!

Over the course of the next few days, the third floor of Seasons began to fill up. Since Sasha and Misty were two of the first contestants to arrive, they greeted all the newcomers, giving them the 411 on the resort and pointing out some of the best spots on the beach.

"Tomorrow is the big day," Misty was saying as they finished off their dinner on the terrace of her room.

"Yeah, I'm trying not to think about it. I just hope it's nothing like *Hell's Kitchen,* where you are screamed at every five minutes, or are told 'you're fired' like on *The Apprentice.*"

Misty laughed. "I know. All of those reality shows make losing look so awful. Viewers always get the shot of the losers driving off alone in the limo, or packing up their knives or dragging their suitcases behind them."

They giggled.

"Or…how 'bout this one? 'Sasha, how about singing your parting song?'"

"Ohhh, yesss." Misty slapped her thigh. "Isn't that awful? The final slap in the face. Sometimes I wish one of those Idols would say 'Go to hell, I ain't singing!' And stomp off the stage."

"Now that would make for some *real* reality television."

"That's what I'm talking about." Misty sipped on her mimosa.

"I've been trying to imagine what this reality show is going to be. What kind of crazy things they're going to make us do. We're the guinea pigs, so to speak."

"Hmmm, true," Misty agreed. "We'll be the first contestants. But as long as I don't have to eat worms or dive off a cliff strapped to a motorcycle, I'm good," she joked.

Sasha roared with laughter. "Girl, you're crazy." She rose from her reclining position on the lounge chair and stretched. "I'm going to turn in. They want us assembled in the lobby at six." She reached for her tray. "I'll leave this outside the door."

"Thanks." Misty got up, too. She followed Sasha to the door. "Hey, listen…"

Sasha turned.

"Just in case…you know, we wind up on opposite sides of the fence in the next few days, I hope we can still be friends."

Sasha smiled. "So do I." She paused a moment. "See you tomorrow."

"'Night." Misty closed the door behind her.

By 5:00 a.m. Sasha had taken her swim in the ocean and returned to her room. She still had an hour to go before they were all to meet downstairs in the lounge. It was a little too early to knock on Misty's door, so she decided to call room service and order a quick breakfast before heading downstairs.

She'd barely slept through the night. She'd tossed and turned, her mind filled with what the day might bring. Although she had seen many reality television shows, she'd never seen one that dealt with hotels. Especially not one entitled *Heartbreak Hotel*. She had no idea what was going to be expected of any of them, nor of how to prepare. All she could do was her best. As she sat on the terrace and watched the sun rise over the ocean, she sipped her juice and imagined what it would be like to run her very own hotel.

She knew exactly what she wanted. The resort would cater to people who had a special interest in reclaiming their health and finding balance in their lives while enjoying all the amenities of a full-service spa, as well as exercise and nutrition programs. She wanted it to be accessible to everyone.

She'd spent her entire life in the South, but she was willing to relocate if that was what was necessary in order to make her dream come true. The grand prize for the competition was owning and operating a hotel. There had been no indication in the reality show rules about where that hotel would actually be. For all she knew it could be right here in Antigua. And although she didn't have many qualms about moving somewhere else in order to have her dream come true, living on a Caribbean island was a little bit more than she'd bargained for.

There was no use in speculating, she thought. The contest finale was more than two weeks away. Anything could happen during that time. The first thing she'd have to do was size up her competition—and figure out how she could get rid of them one by one. Just thinking about eliminating the competition made her cringe. It wasn't in her nature to be cutthroat. But she knew that in this kind of contest, if it was anything like other reality shows that she'd watched on television, it was every man and every woman for themselves.

She checked her watch. It was 5:45 a.m. She rose from the lounge chair and returned to the bedroom. Everything she needed for the day she'd already put in her bag.

The letter from the *Heartbreak Hotel* producers had made it very clear that once the competition began, everything that the contestants did would be taped for television, with a little editing of course. With that in mind, she made a quick dash to the bathroom, flipped on the light and checked her makeup. Adding an extra dash of lipstick, and then taking a look at herself in the full-length mirror behind the door. Once she was satisfied with her appearance, she headed out.

She hoped she didn't look too casual, she thought as she headed toward the elevator. She'd spent most of the morning deciding exactly what to put on. Everyone always said that white made you look heavier. Dark colors were totally out of the question. After all, this was a tropical island. She'd eventually settled on her favorite yellow-and-aqua sundress and her white flip-flops.

By the time she made her way down to the lounge several of the contestants and the entire camera crew had arrived. She looked over the small gathering to see if she could catch sight of Misty. She spotted her way up in the front having a very intimate conversation with one of the cameramen. Sasha smiled and shook her head then found a seat on the sidelines. Here she would be out of the way, but would still have the vantage point of seeing everybody who came in and out.

In no time the room was filled with all of the contestants and all of Heartbreak Hotel honchos.

Two men and two women took their places at the front of the room behind the long table. As they took their seats the room grew quiet. All eyes were on the four people at the front of the room. That is, until a late-comer drew everyone's attention to the entrance way.

Sasha's gasp was so loud she was sure that everybody in the room heard her. Her body heated so quickly she felt as if she would combust. Sweat broke out across her forehead. This could not be happening.

Mitchell glanced quickly around the room and found an empty seat close to the door. Sasha wanted to crawl into a ball and roll out of the room unseen by all of the people there. Especially Mitchell Davenport. What in the world was he doing here? He *couldn't* be one of the contestants. Was he with the show? Someone from the studio? Her head began to pound. She just wanted this moment to be over. Before he noticed her.

What the hell is she doing here? It took all of Mitchell's concentration to keep from staring at Sasha. Or rather, from throwing daggers at her with his eyes. Is this where she had sneaked off to? All he wanted to know was why had she left without a word. He clenched and unclenched the muscles in his jaw until he felt a headache coming on.

He could barely concentrate on what the man at the front of the room was saying to them—something about everybody getting hooked up with microphones and doing their first audio interview.

Were he and Sasha going to be competitors? If so, he would take great pleasure in beating her. She'd made a fool out of him. And he had had about all he could take of women and their own personal agendas.

All of the contestants were asked to line up so they could come up and do their audio presentation. Sasha's entire body was trembling. Misty eased up behind her and got on line.

"Hey girl," she whispered. "How's it going?"

Sasha could barely get the words together to tell Misty exactly what was going on. "Um, remember when I gave you that hypothetical situation where you met a guy and you really couldn't tell him what was going on and you have to make a choice?"

Misty frowned and then nodded. "Yeah, what about it?"

"Well, it was not hypothetical."

"What are you talking about?"

"That guy…that I didn't know that well…? He's here."

"What?" Misty screeched.

"Sssh."

"Okay, okay. He's here? You're kidding me."

Sasha moved up the line and Misty scooted right behind her. "No. I'm not kidding. He just walked in, right before the orientation began."

"Damn, girl, how did that happen?"

Sasha threw a look at Misty over her shoulder and rolled her eyes. "Do I look like I have the answer to that question?"

"Sorry. But you have to admit, it *is* kind of crazy."

"What am I going to do?"

"Which one is he?"

"Don't look now. I'm going to describe him to you. He's tall, about six-two. Chocolate-brown. He has on a white T-shirt, black jeans and dark shades."

"Dang, girl, he sounds good enough to eat."

"You are not helping the situation, Misty," Sasha said between clenched teeth.

"Can I look now?"

"Wait until you get all the way up front. He has to be at the end of the line. I refuse to look behind me and have him catch me staring. And you better not stare either."

"Okay, okay."

"I don't know how I'm going to be able to concentrate on whatever those people up there ask me when I know he's right back there."

"You'll do just fine. Just remember why you're

here. And remember, he's obviously here for the same reason you are. And me too for that matter."

"You sound just like my friend April. That's exactly what she would've told me."

"Great minds think alike." Misty laughed.

Sasha was the next person up. She stepped in front of the four judges and took a seat. A young girl from the camera crew came up beside her and patted her nose and forehead with a makeup sponge then dashed away. The judges introduced themselves—Charlotte Moss, Devin Williams, Brian Hamilton, Grace Edwards.

Charlotte was the spokesperson and gave Sasha her instructions.

"I'd like you to state your name, your age, what city you're from and what you hope to accomplish in this competition. How does that sound?"

"Sounds easy enough," Sasha said. "I'm sure it'll be the easiest part of the competition." All four of the judges laughed, which eased the knot in Sasha stomach.

"Whenever you're ready, Ms. Carrington, just look directly into the camera and begin," Charlotte directed.

Sasha nodded. She looked into the camera, drew in a deep breath and began speaking. Before she knew it, she was done—it wasn't as difficult as she'd thought it was going to be. But when she got up and turned around, her gaze connected with Mitchell's. Her heart slammed in her chest. The look of pure anger that lit up his dark eyes was directed at her. The only way to get out of the room was to walk past him. Maybe the floor would open up and swallow her, but, of course, in the real world things like that didn't happen. In the real world, you have to deal with the consequences of your actions.

Maybe she should wait a couple of minutes until Misty was finished and they could walk out together. That way she could pretend that she hadn't seen him, or at the very least that she hadn't recognized him. And maybe he would do the same.

While she debated what her next move should be, Mitchell's attention was drawn by the young man standing in front of him in line. Sasha seized the opportunity and hurried out of the door. She practically ran across the lobby, wanting to put as much distance between her and Mitchell as quickly as possible.

What was she going to do? She obviously couldn't hide from him forever. Sooner or later they were going to have to confront each other. She knew she owed him an explanation, but now that they were both here it should be obvious to him why she hadn't told him where she was going.

The more she thought about it, the more she realized that she should be just as pissed off at him as he was at her. He'd never told her his real reasons for being in Antigua. Just that he was on some "business."

She knew the orientation wasn't over, and at some point, she was going to have to go back. She returned to the lounge. Peering over the heads and shoulders of everyone in the room she looked desperately for Misty. Once again, she saw her off in the corner in deep conversation with one of the cameramen.

"So do you plan to run off from here, too?"

Sasha's heart thumped in her chest. Slowly she turned around to face the voice that came from behind her. "If you're here, then you know the reason why I couldn't say anything."

"You could've said something…'Goodbye'… 'See ya later.' If I'd known it was going to be a one-night stand I would've left some money on the dresser."

The sound of the slap was like a gunshot. Everyone within earshot gasped in unison. Sasha didn't care. She'd never been so humiliated in her life. He was calling her nothing more than a whore. She didn't know whether to scream or to cry, but it was no one's fault but her own. This was a mess she'd gotten herself into. She should've known better than to follow her instincts. She shouldn't have allowed her attraction to Mitchell to outweigh her judgment. Now she was paying for that in the most public of ways.

Mitchell rocked his jaw from left to right. He wouldn't give Sasha the satisfaction of responding. He walked away and took a seat on the other side of the room. No one dared ask him what was going on.

Tears burned in her eyes, but she refused to cry. She stood stock-still and leaned up against the wall, staring at nothing, reliving the moment over and over again. How was she going to manage to get through this competition? She didn't think she could do it. Maybe she should just let the judges know now, back out while she still had the opportunity.

"What in the world was that about?" Misty said.

Sasha hadn't even seen Misty come up to stand in front of her. She blinked to focus. "What?" she asked, sounding confused and dazed.

"I asked you, what in the world just happened? You slapped the mess out of him. What did he say to you?"

In stilted stops and starts Sasha replayed what Mitchell had said to her only moments ago.

"Wow. He was probably just upset."

"There was no reason for him to say that to me." Sasha thought about it for a moment. What choice had she given him?

"So what are you gonna do?"

Sasha drew in a breath and took in the room around her. She'd come too far to turn around or to be turned around by something she no longer had any control over. Let Mitchell think what he wanted to think. There was no hope for them at this point anyway, not after his comment and her reaction. Whatever possibility there may have been was over.

"I'm gonna continue with this competition. That's what I came here for."

"That's more like it. I'm going to enjoy kicking your butt," Misty said, laughing.

"In your dreams, sister."

After all the ten contestants had completed their mini interviews, the judges explained what the next few days would entail. They showed a slide show of the hotel which they would be rehabbing. Sounds of alarm bubbled up from all of the contestants. The hotel looked as if it had been condemned and there was no way that anyone could believe that in two weeks they could restore it to its former glory.

"You will all be judged obviously on your competitive nature but also on your instincts, your ability to think on your feet and out of the box. Over the next couple of weeks you will be asked to do things you've probably never done before. You're going to have to develop a budget. You're going to have to get a construction crew. You're going to have to design, decorate, hire staff and get that hotel ready for guests in a matter of two weeks."

A collective groan rippled through the room.

Misty leaned over and whispered to Sasha, "They have got to be kidding."

"I don't think so."

After the slide show the judges instructed them to return to their rooms to get whatever they would need for the rest of the day, make sure they had on comfortable clothes and shoes and be ready to get on the bus in the next hour.

"Guess I should change out of my trying-to-be-cute outfit," Misty said, drawing laughter from Sasha.

"You and me both. Come on, let's go change."

Sasha was pleased to see that they would be traveling on a real bus equipped with a bathroom, television and, yes, air-conditioning, and not another hot and bumpy six-passenger van. When she boarded the bus, she saw that Misty had already grabbed a seat near the back and saved one for her. As she walked toward Misty she didn't notice Mitchell on the bus, at least not at first. If there was any justice in the world, maybe he'd pack up his bags and decided to go back to wherever it was he *really* came from. No such luck—the moment she sat down she glanced up at the doorway and there he was. He noticed her too and took the first available seat—the one directly behind the driver.

"It suddenly got very chilly in here," Misty said.

"Very funny."

Charlotte stood at the front of the bus and tapped on the microphone to get everyone's attention.

"Hi, everybody. I just want to give you a few instructions before we take off," Charlotte said. "If for any reason somebody gets separated from the group, we are to meet back at the bus at 7:00 p.m. sharp. The bus will bring us back here to Seasons. I must warn you that the hotel is in the middle of nowhere. The only way in or out is by car. So please, whatever you do, don't wander off, and always travel with a partner."

"Geez, sounds creepy if you ask me," Misty said under her breath.

"I hope this doesn't turn into one of those B movies," Sasha added.

Misty giggled. She looked around at the passengers on the bus. "Hey, did you notice that there are five men and five women?"

"I'm not sure I really paid it any attention."

"During the competition, you'll be working in groups and pairs and individually," Brian announced, speaking for the first time since he was introduced earlier in the morning. "And the judges will be evaluating you on a variety of skills and perfor-

mances. Every time you step into Heartbreak Hotel
you will be filmed and everything that you say will
be recorded. I want you all to be aware of that."

"Are you ready for this?" Misty asked Sasha.

"I don't have any choice now. It's too late to
turn back."

"Your first assignment for today will be to clean
the entire facility."

Sasha shrugged. "How bad could it be?"

About a half hour later, the bus slowed and
pulled up in front of the hotel, or at least what was
left of it. One by one the crew and contestants
stepped off the bus and formed a line in front of the
hotel. Groans of disbelief circled around the gathering. What once had been a magnificent hotel was
now no more than a relic from a scary horror movie.
The paint was peeling, windows were broken. The
doors were hanging off the hinges. Whatever the
landscape once had been, was now totally unrec-
ognizable. Birds had taken up residence on the roof
and were looking at the people on the ground.

"Oh my goodness," Sasha moaned. "They can't
be serious."

"This place looks like it hasn't been used since
the 1800s."

"Can I have everyone's attention?" Charlotte
said. "It is now 8:30 a.m. We will be working here

in the hotel until 7:00 p.m. You will be broken up into two groups. One group will work the east wing. The second group will work the west wing. All of the supplies you'll need to begin getting the hotel in shape are inside. The team that does the best by the end of the day will get a special prize."

"When I call your name," Brian said, "please step to my right."

Brian began calling names. Mitchell was in the first group called up. Sasha held her breath hoping that they wouldn't be on the same team. *Maybe in Antigua wishes do come true,* she thought, as she was selected for group two along with Misty.

"Okay, everybody," Charlotte said. "Let's get started. Good luck everybody."

She led the groups indoors. The outside of the rundown hotel couldn't compare to the devastation of the inside.

"This place doesn't need a cleanup team so much as a demolition squad," Misty said.

Sasha looked around and sadly shook her head. She couldn't imagine how they could ever get this place in shape by the end of the day. It just wasn't possible.

"Team one will take the west wing," Brian announced. "Team two will take the east wing."

"Each wing has three floors," Charlotte said. "Eight bedrooms on either side, and a master suite

on either side. There are two full kitchens on the
ground level and two dining rooms with a bar.
That is your challenge for today. The camera
crews will be following everything that you do,
and, as I mentioned earlier, everything you say
will be recorded. Okay folks, let's get started."
She checked her watch. "Let's meet back here at
one o'clock for lunch."

On either side of the dilapidated reception desk
everything they needed to get started was piled
up. Buckets, brooms, mops, disinfectant, rubber
gloves, garbage bags and everything in between.
All of the contestants began gathering items and
headed off to their designated work areas.

"I suggest that each of us take one of the bedrooms to get started," Sasha said. "Just like housekeeping does at any hotel."

"We can start on the top floor and work our
way down," another group member suggested.

"Good idea," Misty said. "Let's get started."

They worked in earnest for the next few hours,
and by the time they broke for lunch they had suc-
cessfully cleaned five of the eight bedrooms while
the camera crew had recorded their every move.

By the time they crawled back on the bus and
sat down for lunch, everyone was groaning in
agony. Sasha immediately noticed that Mitchell
looked a little worse for wear. That small degree

of satisfaction put a smile on her face. Maybe he wasn't so tough after all.

Mitchell ate his lunch in silence. Periodically he would snatch a look in Sasha's direction. It didn't go unnoticed by him that she looked like she had barely broken a sweat the entire morning. *She was probably busy giving orders,* he thought, *instead of working like the rest of her teammates.* He was still smarting from that smack she'd given him earlier at the hotel. Maybe he *had* been a little harsh with what he'd said to her, he thought, as he chewed on his sandwich. But she didn't leave him much choice, not with the way she'd simply walked out without a word. What was he supposed to think? He glanced up and realized that she was staring at him. In that instant, before she tore her gaze away, he could've sworn he saw sadness in her eyes. Or maybe it was regret. In any case, they were on opposite sides. And that's the way it was going to stay. Let the best man, or woman, win. He finished off his sandwich, washed it down with a bottle of water and hopped off the bus and back out into the blazing afternoon sun. He was ready to get back to work and stay as far away from Sasha as humanly possible.

Chapter 10

By the time six-thirty rolled around and the judges began announcing that there was a half hour left before the final review, Sasha's body was aching so badly she didn't think she'd be able to move another muscle.

"This day can't be over soon enough for me," Sasha groaned as she tugged a bucket of water behind her.

"I think we did pretty good," Misty huffed as she loaded a bag of garbage onto the cart.

"I wonder how the other team did," Tina, another team member, asked.

"We'll find out soon enough," mumbled Mark, a teammate bringing up the rear.

"We never did make it down to the kitchen," Sasha said. "I wonder if the other team did."

"At least we got all of the bedrooms done, and the halls and bathrooms," Tina said as they began heading for the stairs.

Tina was barely five feet tall, and if she weighed a hundred pounds, it was a miracle. But she worked like two grown men, putting the entire team to shame with the amount of work she was able to accomplish. If they did win today's challenge, they would owe it in part to Tina.

Both teams were assembled on the ground floor in front of the reception desk. The four judges stood in front of them.

"You've had a very successful day," Charlotte began. "Both teams did a phenomenal job with the challenge that was presented to you. However, as you all know, only one team can win each challenge."

"So, for now," Devin began, "everybody can get back on the bus, we'll head over to the hotel, and the judges will review the tapes for the day. At nine o'clock, we'll call everyone back down to the lounge and announce the winner of today's challenge."

All of the contestants excitedly looked at each other and began talking at once.

Charlotte held up her hands to quiet the chatter.

"I know everybody is achy, tired and hungry. So let's get on the bus and head back to the hotel. I'm sure all of you, just like us, want to know who won this competition. The sooner we get back, the sooner we'll find out."

They began filing out. By the time they were on the road for five minutes, everyone was fast asleep.

When Charlotte's voice seeped into Sasha's consciousness and she opened her eyes, she could barely move. Every muscle in her body screamed in agony. Even her eyelashes hurt. Through bleary eyes she looked out of the window and realized that they'd returned to the Seasons Hotel.

"I'm not getting up," Misty groaned. "I can't move. I swear I can't."

"Well, we can't stay here forever. And if I don't get into a shower and some steamy hot water soon, I know I'll never be able to walk again," Sasha moaned.

They helped each other out of their seats and struggled down the narrow aisle of the bus. The excitement of earlier in the day was gone, replaced by silence punctuated by moans and groans about aching muscles.

Somehow Sasha managed to get back to her room and made it a point to avoid eye contact with Mitchell who was entering his room down the hall.

She didn't know what forces of nature were in play that kept them tugging at one another, but when she turned to snatch a glance in his direction, he was staring right at her.

A flutter beat in the bottom of her stomach. She wanted to tell him how sorry she was, how important the time they had spent together was to her, that she hadn't been able to stop thinking about him.

But the moment was gone. He opened his door and disappeared inside.

Sighing, Sasha walked into her room and locked the door behind her. She dropped her purse in the chair and kicked off her shoes. She didn't want her clothes to touch anything in the room. She peeled everything off and left them in a pile in the corner, then immediately went to the shower.

Afterward, feeling almost human, she applied lotion to her body and massaged her feet before getting dressed. A T-shirt and a pair of shorts would have to do for dinner, she thought as she painfully put on her clothes.

She pulled her hair away from her face and put it in a ponytail. She didn't have the strength to do much more. Just as she'd put on a hint of lip gloss, she heard a knock at her door.

Expecting Misty, she pulled the door open and nearly leaped back in surprise at finding Mitchell standing there, his dark eyes glowering at her.

The pulse in her throat beat so rapidly she couldn't swallow.

"What are you doing here?"

"I could ask you the same question, but the answer is obvious. That's not why I came."

"Then…what is it?"

Before she could catch her breath, he snaked his arm around her waist, pulled her hard against him and took her mouth. He backed her up into her room and kicked the door shut behind him.

Sasha's thoughts and libido raced. Was this really happening? She wrapped her arms around him, sighing against his mouth. The elation she felt at holding him again, knowing that he wanted her, had forgiven her, made her heart ache with joy. One large hand grabbed her plump bottom and pressed her flush against his pulsing erection, the other pushed up her shirt above her bra and caressed her breasts with a tenderness that caused her inner thighs to tremble. Sasha moaned with pleasure. He took her hand and placed it on his rock-hard center. A growl of urgent need rumbled in his throat. He sucked in air between clenched teeth.

Then, just as suddenly as he'd appeared on her doorstep, he let her go. She stumbled backward, dazed and confused, when he stepped away from her. His fierce gaze rolled up and down her body. She felt suddenly naked and extremely vulnerable.

Without a word he turned and walked out of the door, leaving it standing open.

For several moments she stood trembling from head to toe. It wasn't until she heard the sound of voices approaching her door that she came back to herself. She glanced down at her disheveled appearance and hurried toward the door to close it, pulling her shirt back down into place.

Was that whole episode a way to humiliate me? she wondered miserably, pressing her back against the door. Briefly she shut her eyes as a tremor ran along her spine. If so, then he'd succeeded. She felt like a fool, a cheap fool.

She drew in a shaky breath. He'd never have the chance to do it again. He'd gotten his licks in, he'd seen that he still had some power over her, but no more.

If it was a battle of wills he wanted, that was exactly what he was going to get. From here on out it was strictly business. Any notion of reconciliation was off the table. He'd made his position clear: he didn't think much of her. That little performance wasn't about caring or need, it was about power. Well that was about to change.

Pure fury coursed through Mitchell's veins. And it wasn't directed at Sasha. It was directed at himself.

He was furious with himself for being so weak, for allowing his feelings to control his actions.

He should never have kissed or touched her or allowed her to feel how much he wanted her. He should have let her go on thinking she had the upper hand when she'd slapped him for his crude remark. Now she was sure to see the power she had over him, so much so that he couldn't control his hunger for her anytime she was in the vicinity.

How in the hell did he expect to get through this competition if he couldn't keep his mind and his hands off her?

He paced the confines of his room. It seemed to shrink smaller and smaller as his anxiety grew. Finally he pushed open the sliding doors of his terrace and stepped outside, hoping that the cool evening breeze would lower his internal temperature.

He leaned against the railing. No matter how hard he tried he couldn't seem to get her off of his mind. He'd tried. He'd tried with Joy Martin. They'd spent most of the evening together, back at Jolly Beach Resort and all of the following morning, and it was clear to him that she wanted to take things to the next level. She'd said as much:

"Listen, Mitch. I'm a big girl, just here to have a good time." She'd run her finger along his chest as they'd sat knee to knee at the table in the dining room. "I'd love for you to spend the night with me.

No strings. Just some fun between consenting adults." She ran her tongue slowly across her lips and took her bare foot and placed it gently on his crotch, making him jump at her bold move. She flashed a sly smile as she massaged him with her toes. "I know it will be worth your while."

For a moment he'd considered heartily agreeing with her offer. She was easy on the eyes, had a great body. She was fun, smart and willing. What more could a man ask for? But he couldn't. As much as he'd tried to be turned on by Joy, he simply wasn't. Whatever that "thing" was, it simply wasn't there for him. At least not with her. And it wasn't that she didn't turn him on, she did…but just barely. With Joy he felt like a car that was running on fumes and just coasting along. But with Sasha he was in overdrive, engines revved and ready to go. The last thing he needed was to be lying in bed with Joy trying to explain why he couldn't make it to the finish line.

He'd reached under the table and lowered her foot to the floor. "I think you're great. I really do. But this isn't what I'm looking for. Not right now, anyway." He'd pushed back from his seat and stood. Joy watched him in wide-eyed disbelief. "If you want I'll walk you back to your room."

Her eyes narrowed, and she'd angled her head to the right, a coy smile on her lips. "Who is she?"

"What?"

"Who is she? The woman who has you wrapped around her finger?"

Mitchell rocked his jaw from side to side. "Is it that obvious?"

"Let's put it this way, the last time a man turned me down it was because he couldn't get another woman out of his system."

Mitchell half laughed. "I'm really sorry. I don't want you to think that I was leading you on. It wasn't that way at all."

Joy stood up. She came around the table and stood very close in front of him. She gazed up into his eyes. "She's a lucky woman, whoever she is."

Well if she's the lucky one, what does that make me? Mitchell thought miserably, turning away from the memories of that conversation to the lull of the ocean rushing to the shore.

He grabbed his room card key from the nightstand. It was past time for him to get "unwrapped" from Sasha's pretty little fingers.

All of the contestants had assembled in the lounge that had been assigned to them. Of course, members of the two groups banded with their teammates, exchanging comments, hoots of laughter, ridicule and words of assurance about which team had won.

Mitchell was content to sit as far away from Sasha as possible after the spectacle he'd made of himself. He folded his arms tightly across his chest and fixed his hard stare on the four judges, staying out of the fray and away from any conversation that wasn't directed specifically at him.

After a long conversation with herself in the bathroom mirror, Sasha had picked up her self-confidence, draped it around her shoulders like a cape and walked with confidence into the room that buzzed with conversation and activity. No one had to know how small she really felt, not if she held her head high and kept a positive smile on her face and a light in her eyes. As her mother had always reminded her and her sister, Tristan, *When you wear your feelings on your sleeve, your emotions are there for the picking.* It was one of her mother's many sayings that Sasha had heard but never put much stock in until now. They could pry her open with a crowbar and she'd never again let Mitchell Davenport know how she felt.

Over a few bobbing heads, she spotted Misty way up front. She walked around the row of seats and sat down two seats away from Misty and next to Tina. Misty was deep in a conversation with Mark. Sasha had spied Mitchell sitting along the far wall when she came in, and for a moment her emotions softened. For all of his tough demeanor and rigid body language, he appeared totally alone in a room full of people.

But she couldn't let the momentary impression of his vulnerability cloud her judgment. She settled back into her seat just as the lights dimmed and the four judges made their way to the front of the room.

"I hope everyone had a chance to unwind for a bit," Charlotte began, bringing the room to silence. "Tonight we make our first major decision of this competition and I must warn you it will only get more difficult from here. But before I scare you all off, let's take a look at both teams as you were being filmed earlier today."

A huge projection screen was lowered from the ceiling. The *Heartbreak Hotel* logo—a red-and-white hotel with an arrow running through it—flashed on the screen, followed by the procession of the contestants onto the bus for the ride to hotel hell.

Watching the day unfold once again brought as many groans as the actual work. The camera crew was certainly good at their job. They caught every dispute, captured the frenzied activity of the contestants, and they had even caught one worker fast asleep in the closet of a room that was supposedly being cleaned, which brought a roar of laughter. It was clear from the videotape who the real workers were. Both teams had made substantial progress in getting the hotel into shape, so it was hard to tell from the contestants' perspective who the real winners were. Both sides claimed victory.

After about twenty minutes of watching the videotape, Charlotte stepped up to the mike and turned off the tape.

"Before I announce today's winners, I want to say to each and every one of you that you've all done a fantastic job today. The decision was a difficult one. The judges debated long and hard to come up with today's winner. The winner of today's challenge is…group A."

One side of the room erupted in applause. Sasha and Misty gave each other stunned looks. They couldn't believe that they had not won.

"Congratulations to group A. Your prize is an all-expenses-paid evening out on the town in St. John's and the day off tomorrow. The losers, group B, will return to the hotel tomorrow to complete all of the work that was left undone today."

Brian took over the microphone. "Because this is the first challenge, there will be no individual eliminations. However, after the next challenge, the group that loses will be required to select one member of their group to go home."

Moans and groans filtered across the room. The members of group B cut deadly looks at Mark, the culprit found sleeping in one of the closets.

"Thank you, everyone," Charlotte said. "Congratulations to group A. I suggest that group B get some rest. You have a long hard day ahead of you tomorrow. We'll be pulling out at 7:00 a.m. sharp."

Misty uttered a string of expletives as the defeated team rose and began heading out to shouts of victory coming from the opposite side of the room.

"I can't believe it," Tina said.

"Now we know where Mark was for an hour while we were busting our behinds," Misty groused. "I think I'm going to stop by the bar before heading upstairs," she said to Sasha and Tina.

"I'll join you," Tina said.

"I'm going to bed," Sasha said. "See you all in the morning."

They parted ways and Sasha walked toward the elevator. When she arrived on her floor her breath caught harshly in her chest. Mitchell was standing at the end of the corridor, looking her way, almost as if he was waiting for her to show up.

Her hands began to shake when she tried to slide the key card in the slot. It fell from her fingers, landing on the carpet below. Her thoughts and her heart raced out of control. The overwhelming sensation of approaching danger, something unseen, only felt, wrapped around her like mist and clung to her skin.

She yelped in outright fear when the heat of another presence hovered over her body, reached down, retrieved her fallen card and slid it through the slender opening. The soft beep of the door releasing sent another wave of anxiety racing through her. Was he going to push his way into her room, finish what he had started?

Mitchell handed her the card without a word, turned and walked down the hallway to his room.

Sasha, still caught in the surreal moment, couldn't get her brain to make her legs move. Finally, the sound of others getting off the elevator snapped her back to reality.

She hurried inside her room, locking and double-locking her door. Her hands shook and her knees wobbled. She collapsed in the chair by the bed and covered her face with her hands.

She could still feel him all over her. The heat of his body warmed her chilled insides. His fingers had grazed hers when he'd reached for the key card and the touch was incendiary.

This couldn't go on. It was insane. If she didn't know better she'd think she was possessed by some nymph that refused to be exorcised.

Her cell phone rang. She dug in her bag, pulled it out and stared at the number. She drew in a breath of cheer and pushed it out.

"Hey, sis. How are you?"

"Calling to check on you. How's the vacation going?"

Tristan sounded remarkably cheerful for a woman who'd recently walked out on her husband. Sasha got up from the chair and stretched out across the bed, tucking a pillow behind her head. Maybe some of her sister's good spirits would rub off on her.

"Pretty good. The weather is great."

"So why do you sound like that?"

"Like what?"

"Like you have something on your mind that you don't want to talk about."

Sasha shut her eyes for a moment. Tristan knew her too well. It came from spending years with a person and sharing secrets in the dark when you were supposed to be asleep, covering for each other when trouble from their parents, teachers or friends was on the horizon. But Sasha was still so accustomed to being the big sister, the protector, the fixer, she was having trouble wrapping her head around the notion that Tristan was a grown-ass woman, and maybe it was time for the roles to be reversed. She could use an ear, an opportunity to unburden the thoughts that were rolling around in her head.

"Well…"

By the time Sasha was finished telling her sister about Mitchell Davenport, she felt tons lighter. She didn't leave anything out, other than the real reason why she was in Antigua.

"Damn, girl, let you off the ranch for a minute and look what happens."

Sasha bust out laughing. That's what she needed—a good laugh to release the bands of tension that tugged at the back of her neck and across her shoulders.

"Whew," Sasha sputtered, getting herself together, and wiping tears of laughter from her eyes, "you haven't lost your sense of humor."

"Had to hold on to something, sis," Tristan said, a hint of pain tainting her words.

"I know." A moment of understanding silence hung between the sisters. "Enough about me, how are you?"

"Better each day. Some days are better than others, but I'm taking them one at a time, ya know? This breakup was a long time coming. I didn't want to see the signs, but they were there. We try to hold on to what's familiar even if it's not good for us. It's just easy. The devil you know..." she added, citing the old adage. "But the real juicy story isn't me, it's you, girl. I may not be an expert on men, but from everything you've told me, that man has a serious thing for you, and you have one for him. I'm not getting what the problem is. There's definitely something you're not telling me."

Sasha turned on her side and tossed around the idea of telling her sister the whole story. She would find out soon enough, she reasoned. And Tristan was one of the best secret keepers she knew—next to April.

"Okay, look, I'm gonna tell you something and you betta not say a word!"

"Pinky swear," Tristan said, reverting to their childhood promise of secret loyalty.

"Is Mom anywhere around?" Sasha asked, whispering as if their mother could hear her.

"No," Tristan whispered back. "They're upstairs asleep," she said, referring to her parents.

"Okay." Sasha blew out a long breath. "A few months ago…"

"What!" Tristan's muffled squeal when the story ended tickled Sasha. She knew her sister loved to whoop and holler and having to contain her excitement was killing her.

"Yep, so that's why I'm here. They're filming everything for the show that will air this fall. If I win, sis, I get my own resort, a budget, my dream," she added, the taste of possibility sweet on her tongue.

"Wow." Tristan strung out the word until it was almost three syllables. "You *have* to win. I know how much you want to do your own thing. You've been talking about it for years. Mom will miss you, but you have to do you, sis."

"Thanks," Sasha whispered, feeling the enormous weight lifted from her shoulders. "I should have told you a long time ago."

"Well, I'll try not to be hurt by the slight," Tristan teased. "But back to your dilemma. On top of everything else, now the two of you are on opposing teams?"

"Yep."

"Humph, humph, humph. That's going to be sticky."

"I want to win this thing. In the ideal world, I'd love a shot at a relationship with Mitchell. But the way things are between us, I can't tell if he likes me or hates me."

"Look, what are you and April always telling me? Put your cards on the table, right? So go over there—wear something sexy—and tell him what's on your mind. Either he'll make mad, passionate love to you, or he'll call security and have you kicked out of his room."

Sasha giggled. "Now that would be a major news item."

"For real," Tristan singsonged. "But seriously, until you come clean with what's going on with you, it's only going to get worse the longer the two of you are thrown together with all that hot, steamy lust smoldering between you." She giggled.

"I know. I know. Somehow, if it goes any-where, we're going to have to figure out how to separate our emotions from the competition. I have no intention of letting my feelings for some man derail my dream."

"Just remember what Grandma always said, 'A branch that bends won't break.'"

Sasha considered the wise words and the full implication of their meaning. "I think I'll put on something sexy and make a house call," she finally said.

"More like a booty call," Tristan chuckled.

"Very funny," Sasha said, joining in the laughter. "Thanks for listening, and for the advice."

"You would have figured it out eventually. Now go get your might-be man. Call me," Tristan said before hanging up.

A sunbeam smile stretched across Sasha's full mouth. She pulled herself up from the bed, suddenly energized and focused. She was going to march right over there, knock on his door and tell him a thing or two...three...four. She danced around the room to a calypso beat in her head as she prepared to meet her destiny.

Chapter 11

The feeble tap at Mitchell's door was so faint he thought he might have imagined it. He set his glass of rum and Coke on the glass-and-wrought-iron table and leaned forward, listening. There it was again. He stood, checked his watch. It was nearly midnight, pretty darn late for hotel staff to come knocking. He pushed the glass doors open a bit farther and stepped into the bedroom then crossed to the door.

"Who?"

"Sasha...Carrington," she said softly.

His stomach jerked. He peered through the peephole, and damn if she wasn't standing right there, looking delectable as usual. He frowned. What could she possibly want? With a bit of reluctance he unlatched the door and stood halfway in the small opening, peering down at her.

Sasha sucked in air to stifle the electric shock of coming face-to-face with Mitchell's bare, hard, broad chest. She forced her eyes upward. That wasn't any better. His gaze was stormy. The lips that she remembered doing naughty things to her flesh were pressed into a tight unmovable line. His pajama pants hung low on his hips, the thin line of dark hair leading down to sensual delights peeking out above the band. Her throat was tight and dry and all coherent explanation for her appearance was someplace in her brain that she couldn't access.

"It's late. Is something wrong?" he finally asked, breaking into her trance.

Sasha blinked several times. "Um…I was…"

His brow flicked upward in question.

"I came by here because…" She breathed deeply. "Something very right went very wrong and…"

She never got to finish her sentence. Mitchell's long arm snaked out and drew her across the doorway and into his arms. His mouth sought hers, silencing any explanations and questions. That could all wait. What he needed now was Sasha. He needed her in his arms, in his bed. He needed to bury this longing he had deep inside her so that he could breathe, move through the day seeing colors again instead of black and white. The need roared through him as he lifted her off the floor and carried her to his bed, his lips never leaving hers.

Mitchell lowered her to the bed, hesitating only a moment as he stood above her, giving her this last opportunity to leave, to end this now.

She reached for the buttons of her white cotton midrift blouse and began to unbutton it, letting it fall away to reveal the lace demi-bra underneath. She watched his nostrils flare and his chest heave when his gaze ran hot and heavy across her exposed flesh. She sat up, shrugged off her top and unsnapped the front opening of her bra. The light in his eyes crackled, catching the rays of the moon and stars that streamed in through the glass doors of the terrace.

As if in a trance, Mitchell reached out and tenderly touched the rise of her breasts. His fingers were so feather-light against her skin that she shivered, a sigh escaping her lips. She clasped his hand, pressing it to her. She wanted to feel him.

Mitchell came down beside her on the bed. He caressed her cheek and brushed his thumb across her slightly parted lips before leaning her back, bending, not breaking her to his will. He stretched out beside her and took the tip of her breast into his mouth, laving the sensitized skin, nibbling and sucking until she screamed out his name and the heavenly father for mercy.

"Not tonight," he ground out deep in her ear. "I fully intend to relieve the torture that you've been putting me through since you walked out. Then maybe I can forgive you for making me crazy."

He straddled her, lifted her hips and unceremoniously stripped her of her shorts and barely-there thong, tossing them both to the floor. He pushed her legs apart with a sweep of his knee and settled between her parted thighs.

Her heart hammered in her chest. He stroked her hips up and down in a rhythmic motion, his thumbs gently dipping in and out of the juncture of her thighs coming closer each time to her clit that was pulsing and twitching, begging for his attention. Mitchell was happy to oblige.

When the tip of his tongue flicked across the stiffened bud of her sex, her entire body arched as if shot with a jolt of electric current. She gripped the sheets in her fists and a strangled cry burst from her lips. Her head spun as the intensity grew. He played her like a pianist in concert, up and down the scales, building momentum toward the final crescendo.

Suddenly he pulled away. The heat that had lit her center cooled, and she moaned with longing, her body writhing, searching for release. She opened her eyes to see his exquisite physique silhouetted against the dimness of the room. He rolled a condom over his length, slowly, deliberately, making her wait.

Her heart roared as he moved toward her, lowering himself to her willing and waiting body. He slid his large hands beneath her hips and lifted her center to meet his. His mouth connected with hers in a deep kiss, muffling her sighs as he pushed into the wet velvet warmth.

Was it possible that it was even better the second time? Sasha wondered through the haze of sensations that ran through her. Her flesh was on fire. Her insides pulsed with a life of their own. Mitchell touched her inside and out, leaving no place, no sensation to chance.

As he made love to her, he whispered in her ear things she'd never heard a man tell her before… that she was beautiful, desirable, the kind of woman a man made a life with…

She loved hearing the words, the pillow talk. The big girl in her knew that in the throes of passion people tended to say things they didn't mean, but she would enjoy them for the moment. They both needed to stamp out this lust they had for each other so that they could get busy in the real world. And in the real world they were on opposite sides of the fence. Whether it was love or war, one of them was going to lose.

"Oooh!" she cried out again and again, arching her hips and draping her legs tightly around his broad back. All rational thought vanished when Mitchell hit that spot over and over and sent her spiraling toward heaven.

"You never finished explaining what brought you to my door in the middle of the night," Mitchell cooed against her neck.

Sasha sighed heavily, her body still shimmering from the explosive climax. Why had she come? Was this what she'd expected, what she'd really wanted?

"Honestly?"

"Yes, honestly."

"Well…the truth is, I can't get you out of my head. And I needed to explain to you why I left the hotel without saying anything."

"I'm listening…"

She slowly began to explain about the contract clause, but more importantly her unwillingness to lie to him when she had left, not knowing, of course, that he, too, was a contestant.

"Even more than that…" She hesitated, uncertain about pulling back the curtain on her life and her impression of herself. "I didn't want to wind up being disappointed."

"Disappointed?"

"Yes." She took a deep breath. "The me you see is not the me I was less than a year ago. It took a lot to turn my life around in many ways—family, work, school, my health. I was always the one that was invisible to men. Ms. Dependable to my family. I was the good friend and that was it. But I made a decision to change all of that. And when this opportunity came along I knew it was my one chance to finally do something for me. And I couldn't let anything stand in the way of that." She paused a beat. "Not even meeting you."

Mitchell was silent for so long that Sasha was sure he'd fallen asleep and her big confession had landed on deaf ears.

"I felt the same way," he said into the darkness. "The last thing I was looking for was someone in my life. Especially now. You know why I got so pissed off when you left without a word?"

Sasha turned on her side, curving into his arm. "No, why?"

He told her about Regina.

"We'd been together for almost five years. Lived together for two. I figured she was the one. My restaurant was doing well, and I was even thinking of opening a second one when the bottom fell out. I had to start laying off staff, cut back on supplies, there were fewer and fewer customers. Then I couldn't make the mortgage payments on the restaurant or the house."

She felt his body tense.

He blew out a disgusted breath. "Before I knew it, I'd lost my business and my house and was living in a rental. And at a time when I needed Regina's support the most, she had an 'epiphany.'" He spat the word with disgust. "She couldn't see herself struggling. It wasn't what she'd signed on for, and she knew if we stayed together we'd grow to resent each other and she didn't want that." He snorted a laugh. "What a crock of BS."

She sounds like a real piece of work, Sasha thought. "I'm sorry," she murmured.

"Yeah, me too." He blew out a long, hard breath. "So, when you walked out, even though there was no real long-term commitment, it was like going through it all over again."

"I had no idea."

"No way you could know. I didn't even realize the effect it had on me. Guess it was like post-traumatic stress or something," he said, with a hint of laughter in his deep voice.

"So how did you get hooked up in this competition?"

He chuckled. "Alan, my one friend who didn't disappear when the lights went out, turned me on to it. He practically filled out the application for me."

"Sounds like April."

"They'd be perfect for each other," Mitchell said.

Sasha was thoughtful for a minute. "Where does this leave us? We're still stuck in the same reality."

"Are you willing to separate business from pleasure?" He turned on his side, propped up on his elbow and looked into her eyes.

"Best woman wins?"

"Best man?"

A slow smile bloomed across her mouth. "You, Mr. Davenport, have a deal."

"Why don't we seal it?" he asked, his words as thick as the erection that pressed against her warm thigh.

Chapter 12

Having won the first day, Mitchell's team had the next day off and were taken on an all-day excursion around the island, and even got to meet the prime minister for lunch.

Sasha's team on the other hand, spent the entire day working their fingers to the bone, cleaning and painting the rundown hotel.

At the end of the day, the weary team headed back to their rooms to crash and prepare for the next day.

"I wonder how the other team enjoyed themselves?" Misty said as they rode up on the elevator.

"I'm sure they had a better time than we did," Sasha replied, rotating her stiff neck.

The elevator doors slid open.

"Want to meet for dinner and a drink?" Misty asked as they alighted on their floor.

"Girl, I am too tired to even think straight. I'm going to take a shower and hit the sheets."

"Alone?"

Sasha's head snapped in Misty's direction. "What does that mean?"

"I saw you when you tiptoed out of Mitchell's room this morning." Misty's right brow rose for emphasis.

Sash's cheeks burned with embarrassment. "It's not what you think."

"Really? Hey, listen. You're a big girl. Do your thing. I'm just saying if I noticed, someone else might have as well." She patted Sasha's shoulder. "Rest well," she added before walking down the hall to her room.

Sasha let herself into her room and locked the door behind her. She tossed her bag in the chair next to the dresser and began stripping out of her sticky, sweaty clothes.

Misty was right, Sasha reasoned. She didn't want there to be any impropriety, no reason to disqualify either of them. She would never forgive herself.

Although there was nothing written in their agreement that prohibited contestants from engaging in relationships, for all she knew it could be in the fine print. She sat on the side of the bed and took off her shoes before heading into the shower. She turned on the water full-blast and spent the next twenty minutes under the pulsating spray, thinking and unwinding.

When she emerged from the shower, wrapped in a towel and feeling worlds better, the phone was ringing.

"Hello?"

"Hey, it's Mitch."

Her pulse kicked up a notch and she couldn't stop the smile that moved across her mouth. "Hey, it's Sasha," she teased.

His deep chuckle warmed her.

"Should I ask how your day went?"

"No!" She laughed. "But I'm sure you had the time of your life."

"Definitely can't complain, especially after yesterday. Have you had dinner?"

"I'm too tired to eat." A long yawn escaped her lips confirming her assertion.

"I was hoping to see you…"

"Mitch." She took a breath. "Misty saw me this morning…coming from your room."

He was quiet for a moment. "What did she say?"

"Just that she saw me, and if she did, someone else could have."

"There's nothing against us seeing each other."

"I know, I just don't want anyone to get it twisted…to find some way to use it against us."

"What are you suggesting?"

"Maybe we need to be a little more discreet."

"I see. Hey, you're probably right," he said, his tone suddenly cold and distant.

"Do you?"

"Of course. Listen, I know you must be beat, I'm going to order room service and hit the sheets myself."

Tension fluttered in her stomach. She knew that the conversation had quickly taken a bad turn, but she wasn't sure how to get it back on track. "Okay. See you tomorrow."

"'Night."

Sasha slowly hung up the phone. What had gone wrong? Mitchell had just done a complete three-sixty in ten seconds flat. How could he be against them being discreet—if that was even the reason for his change in attitude?

She sat up from the bed and unwrapped the bath towel then went in search of her nightgown. She was too tired to worry about it tonight. To-morrow, when her head was clear, then they could talk.

As she snuggled deep into her overstuffed pillow, her final thought before drifting off to sleep was that she would not allow what might only be an island fling to derail her dream—no matter what she felt for Mitchell.

Promptly at 7:00 a.m. the following morning the two groups assembled in the lounge. Breakfast was buffet style, and when Sasha arrived a line had already formed at the table. She spotted Mitchell sitting next to one of his teammates, sipping on a cup of coffee. He glanced up, saw her and looked away.

Reflexively she jerked back as if she'd been stung, bumping into Misty who was right behind her.

"Oh, sorry," she stuttered, as she righted herself.

"No problem. I have two feet." Misty laughed. "How are you this morning?"

"Okay."

Misty tipped her head to the side. "You don't sound okay. Something happen?"

Sasha lowered her gaze for a moment then shook her head. "No. Guess I didn't get enough rest. That's all."

Misty laughed lightly. "I don't think I'll ever get enough rest again."

Sasha looked at her and smiled. "I'm starved. Let's fill up before everything is gone."

As they made their way down the food line, Misty said under her breath, "Did you notice that there is the same amount of men as women?"

Sasha took a quick look around. She shrugged. "Your point?"

"Maybe there's something to it. Something more than teams. Could be the great hook-up."

Sasha looked over her shoulder, brow creased in amusement. "The great hook-up?"

"Yeah," Misty replied, bobbing her head. "The show *is* called *Heartbreak Hotel*. I mean there must be a reason and since we're the first to do the show, we have no way of really knowing."

"You're crazy," Sasha chuckled.

"Think about it. By a process of elimination the man and woman left standing get the hotel, the money and the happily-ever-after. It's *The Bachelor*, *Who Wants To Be a Millionaire* and *The Dating Game,* all rolled into one.

"Don't be silly." Sasha began piling fruit, eggs and steamed fish on her plate, then added two biscuits for good measure. If today was anything like the past two she was going to need all the energy she could get.

Tina and Mark had secured a table and waved Misty and Sasha over.

"'Mornin', folks," Sasha greeted, taking a seat.

The groups exchanged pleasantries just as Charlotte entered and walked to the front of the room. She tapped the microphone to get everyone's attention.

"Good morning, everyone! I hope you all had a good night's rest and are ready for today's challenge." She eyed everyone in the room before she continued. "Today each of you will begin to learn what it takes to run a major resort from the ground up. There are no more teams. No one to help you or slow you down. Your success or failure depends on you. Each of you over the course of the rest of the week will be assigned to shadow one of the resort employees, do everything they do, learn everything they know. The selections will be random. And each of the resort employees will be grading you on your performance. And, of course, it will all be filmed. At the end of each night for the rest of the week there will be eliminations until we select the winner."

Murmurs rippled around the room.

"Any questions?" She waited. "Good. Enjoy your meal. You'll be paired up shortly." She stepped away from the mike and briskly left the room.

"This sounds interesting," Misty said.

Tina put down her glass of juice. "I wonder what the dismissal line is going to be. *The Apprentice* has 'You're fired,' *The Biggest Loser* has 'You're not the biggest loser,' *Hell's Kitchen* is something like 'Turn in your apron.'"

"Or your knives," Sasha added, chuckling. She bit into a slice of pineapple and chewed thoughtfully. She looked at her former teammates. "Personally, I don't want to be the one to find out."

"I second that," Misty said, raising her juice glass.

"Good luck to everyone," Sasha said, sincerely, touching her glass to each of theirs.

With breakfast out of the way and the dishes cleared, Charlotte and the judges reappeared, followed by a dozen or more hotel employees. She began the introductions of everyone from management to the housekeeping staff.

"All of you have come here with some level of experience in either a restaurant, hotel or bed-and-breakfast. However, running an entire establishment is quite different. This is your opportunity to learn everything from the ground up. The first half of the day, you will be paired with one of the staff members. When we convene for lunch at 2:00 p.m. you will get your second assignment for the day. When I call your name, please come forward to get your assignment."

One by one the contestants went forward and met their mentors.

"Good luck," Sasha whispered to Misty, taking a moment to squeeze her hand when Misty's name was called.

"Thanks, you too."

Sasha tapped her foot in nervous anticipation as

she waited for her name to be called. Her heart lurched when she heard Mitchell's name. She watched him move forward and shake the hand of a stunning young woman who was the supervisor of the housekeeping staff. A pang of jealousy tugged at her as she watched them walk off together. The young woman was obviously enamored of Mitchell, judging by the way she grinned and looked up at him.

She was so busy staring at them that she missed her name being called. Mark had to nudge her. She quickly rose to her feet to find that she was assigned to the head chef, James Albritton, a middle-aged man who was all business.

Sasha followed James to his office, and they immediately began to work in earnest. Although she'd practically grown up in the kitchen, helping her parents manage Carrington Caterers, it was quite different to be responsible for the menu and food-service staffing for an entire resort complex. Therein was the challenge and Sasha was definitely up to the task, absorbing information like a sponge, from how the menu is determined, what foods are in season, having alternatives on hand and scheduling the wait service to accommodating the myriad room-service requests and disgruntled guests.

She took copious notes and asked many questions, following James around as he gave orders, checked on the food preparation and ordered supplies.

James gave Sasha her first assignment—to verify several deliveries based on their current inventory and then to oversee the lunch service in the main dining hall, making note of any discrepancies and soothing any ruffled feathers.

By the time two o'clock rolled around, her head was spinning with information. She thought she'd done a great job, but it was hard to tell. James Albritton was the consummate professional, strictly business, and she wondered if he had teeth as she had yet to see him smile.

"I hope you learned something," he said as he walked her back to the lounge.

"Yes, I certainly did. I really admire all the work it takes to run a kitchen at a major hotel."

He pursed his lips. "I'm sure you will do fine."

She wasn't sure if that was his stamp of approval or a general observation. "Thank you," she murmured.

He bobbed his head once, turned and walked away.

Sasha released a sigh. She didn't know whether to be encouraged or not. What she did know was that she had done her best, and she hoped it would pay off.

When she stepped through the doors of the lounge the only people there were Mitchell and his sexy instructor. Neither of them acknowledged her presence. She went to the long table that held the refreshments and poured herself a glass of icy-cold lemonade, then found a seat on the opposite side of the room.

One by one the contestants began to arrive. Misty slid into a seat beside her.

"How do you think you did?" Misty asked.

"I think I did pretty good. It's hard to tell from my mentor, though. He wasn't the talkative type. Where did you wind up?"

"The business office." She shrugged. "Not bad. Definitely not rocket science."

They chuckled.

"I see Mitchell seems to be pretty cozy with his mentor," Misty said for only Sasha to hear. "Wonder what kind of grade she's going to give him."

Sasha didn't comment even as she thought the very same thing.

After lunch, everyone got their second assignments and they were told to reconvene after dinner when the first round of eliminations would begin.

Chapter 13

The contestants were all seated around the oval-shaped room. Tension was high and conversation was minimal. Everyone held their collective breath as Charlotte and her team of judges came to the front of the room.

"Good evening, everyone. Today has been a very busy and productive day. I know that each of you learned a great deal and there is much more to do, but someone will not be going forward. The decisions were hard, but after reviewing the tapes and talking with each of your mentors, we have come to a decision." She paused for effect. "There will be two people leaving the competition tonight."

A gasp of surprise filtered around the room.

"Mark Washington and Phyllis Meyers."

The sigh of relief from the remaining contestants was palpable.

"Would you both please come forward?"

Mark got up from his seat and Phyllis, a former teammate of Mitchell's, walked to the front of the room.

"We want to thank you for your participation. We know this is something you both wanted, but the judges have determined that you are not heartbreakers."

"There's the tagline," Misty whispered to Sasha.

"The rest of you still have a chance to win it all," Charlotte continued, not missing a beat. "Be here tomorrow morning at seven for your next assignment."

"Wow," Sasha said to Tina and Misty as they began walking out. "She said one elimination."

"I know," Tina responded. "Which makes me wonder what other tricks they have up their sleeves."

"I wonder why they decided on two people," Misty said.

"To mess with our heads, shake our confidence," Sasha answered. "I'm not surprised about Mark. Not after being caught on tape napping."

The trio giggled.

"He's lucky they didn't can his butt sooner," Misty added.

"But if they can let two go at a time, then the stakes are even higher," Sasha said.

They each stole a look at the other.

"I'm going to head over to the bar for a nightcap," Misty said. "Anyone want to join me?"

"I could use a drink," Tina said. She turned to Sasha. "Coming?"

"No, you two go ahead. I want to make some calls and then I'm going to turn in."

They parted ways and Sasha headed toward the elevator. Mitchell was standing there with his back to her. She started to turn around and head in the opposite direction, but it was as if he sensed her presence and looked over his shoulder.

This time he didn't look away and the tightness began to ease in her chest. She walked toward him as the doors to the elevator opened. He stood aside to let her on.

"Hi," she softly said, walking past him into the enclosed space.

Mitchell stepped in behind her. "How's everything?"

"Good. Tough, but good." She uttered a nervous laugh. "How about you?"

"I feel like I'm back in college cramming for an exam."

Sasha's smile bloomed. "I know exactly what you mean."

The doors closed in front of them. This was the first time they'd been alone since the night they'd spent together. As they stood facing the door, watching the numbers illuminate on the dial, Sasha realized that whatever it was that was going on between them, they seemed to have these one-night stands…at the resort, at Jolly Beach, and now here at Seasons. It was so out of character for her, and she wanted more. More than these clandestine couplings, that left her sizzling and satiated, but emotionally wanting. And she knew the only way to get more was to try to step away from the burning desire that fired her soul every time she thought of him. There had to be more than that. And she believed that Mitchell felt the same way, even if he never said the words.

They stepped off the elevator, and Mitchell waited for Sasha to exit. On the other side of the elevator door she turned to him.

"Do you have a few minutes?"

His dark eyes widened. "Sure."

"My room?"

"Aren't you worried about what someone might think?"

His comment stung, but she wouldn't let it deter her. She lifted her chin. "No. I'm not."

"After you," he said, extending his hand in the direction of her door.

They walked in silence. Sasha felt the muscles in her stomach begin to tighten.

Mitchell leaned casually against the frame of her door as she slid the card through the narrow slot. His body seemed to engulf hers, blocking out the light, leaving only his presence in her view.

She pushed the door open, quickly flipped on the light switch and stepped inside. She walked to the other side of the room, putting some distance between them. Turning, her heart knocked hard in her chest when she took him in; silhouetted by the frame of the door, he resembled the perfect piece of art.

Sasha swallowed. "Do you want to sit on the terrace, maybe order something to drink from room service?"

"Terrace sounds fine. Beautiful night. But the nights are always beautiful in Antigua," he said, taking long, slow strides across the room. He walked past Sasha, pushed open the sliding doors and stepped out into the balmy evening air.

Sasha drew in a breath of resolve and joined him.

"So, what did you want to talk about?" he began right away.

Sasha twisted her hands in front of her then sat down on the lounge chair, which she immediately realized was a mistake. Now she was forced to look up at him. Facing her, he relaxed against the railing.

"I'm not sure where things got off track with us," she began. "But more important, I'm not sure where it's going, or if it's going anywhere at all." She paused to collect her thoughts then slowly stood, in the hopes of leveling the playing field. "What has been going on between us…I've never done anything like this before. It's all new to me. And you probably think all kinds of things about me, but the truth of the matter is, I'm a real regular Southern girl who was given the opportunity to win the prize of a lifetime and on my way…I met you." She laughed sadly. "I've never been any farther from home than New York City for heaven's sake. And here I am all caught up in this torrid…unbelievable, straight-out-of-a-romance-novel relationship with a man I barely know." She looked directly into his eyes. "But the thing is…I *want* to know you." She held up her hand when he started to speak. "Yes, I've been giving mixed signals. But it's not because I'm trying to give you a hard time… I'm trying to work my way through it."

He dipped his head to look at her. "Does this have anything to do with that cute supervisor who was my mentor today?" he teased.

She glanced up, saw the mischief in his eyes, and playfully punched him on the arm. "Not funny.

And no, it has nothing to do with her," she said, her words filled with feigned indignation.

"I think we both have the same problem," Mitchell said. "We both want more than some hot fling on a Caribbean island, some sexy story to tell our friends back home."

"You would tell someone!" she said, appalled.

"I'd change your name, of course." A smile worked at the corners of his mouth.

"You're really asking for it tonight."

He stepped around in front of her and put his arms lightly around her waist, keeping a gentlemanly distance between them. "You know what? Tonight, I'm not asking for anything, except a fresh start. When you told me the other day that you were concerned that someone might see us, I don't know, it rubbed me the wrong way. It resurrected stuff with Regina I haven't quite buried yet. It made me relive how I felt when she couldn't be bothered anymore because things weren't 'what she'd signed up for.' What she really said, and what I've never told anyone, is that she said it would ruin her image if her friends, colleagues and family knew that she was living with someone who had nothing." His half smile was filled with a mixture of anger, sadness and acceptance.

Mitchell looked at Sasha a moment. "It wasn't your fault. Just something I'm still working through, and I will." He drew in a long breath and slowly exhaled. "That was the reason."

Sasha reached out and placed her hand on his hard biceps. "I would never think that. I know it may have sounded callous and…maybe it was in a way." She stumbled around in her head, trying to put together the right words. "I simply didn't want our own basic instincts to jeopardize what we both came here to achieve. If we're going to lose, let it be because we weren't up for the challenge, not because of what goes on behind closed doors."

He nodded his head. "I understand. And you're right. So what made you change your mind? Why invite me to your room?"

"Because unless it's buried in invisible ink on the back of the contract," she stepped closer, "there's nothing saying that we can't be together… if that's what we want."

"Is that what we want?" His thumb teased her chin.

"I say, yes."

"I second that."

"I don't want this competition to come between us, no matter how it turns out," Sasha said, her heart thumping as Mitchell methodically stroked her hip.

"We won't let it."

Her eyes danced across his face. "Hi, my name is Sasha Carrington. I'm from Savannah, Georgia."

"Déjà vu all over again," he joked before kissing her softly.

Mitchell reluctantly eased away before the kiss could build to something more. He held Sasha at arm's length. "As hard…" He frowned. "Poor word choice." Sasha flushed. "As *difficult* as this is for me, I'm going to leave you now and return to my room."

Sasha opened her mouth to protest, and he silenced her with a kiss. "Starting over, remember?"

"Fine," she said, pouting. She folded her arms.

Mitchell chuckled. "You're adorable when you take a stand on something." He kissed the top of her head. "See you in the morning. Get a good night's sleep and I'll take a rain check on the nightcap."

"Deal." She walked with him to the door.

"If we're still left standing after tomorrow's eliminations, how about dinner in town?"

"Love to."

"Great." He turned to leave then stopped. "Good luck tomorrow. I mean that."

"Same to you."

Sasha closed the door behind him and sighed with contentment.

Chapter 14

The following day's competition was just as challenging as the first day's had been. The remaining contestants spent the morning in a classroom learning about vendors, billing, lines of credit and how to place orders for each department of the hotel, from décor to dinnerware. From satellite television and Internet service for the rooms to entertainment for the club.

Sasha's head pounded with information. Even though she'd worked at the Summit Hotel for several years, she'd always been a face at the reservation desk. She'd never been involved in running the hotel, and that was minor in comparison to a resort. Working at the family catering business helped, but it didn't compare to preparing a complex menu for hundreds of people per day.

The remaining eight contestants gathered as they ate their lunch. This was the first time they'd all gotten together since the competition began. It gave them an opportunity to get to know one another outside of the competition.

"So what do you think they'll have us do this afternoon?" Misty asked, looking from one expectant face to the other.

"I was wondering the same thing," Roger, one of Mitchell's former team members, said.

"I'd bet money that it is going to be something physical," Tina said.

"As long as I don't have to paint another house or scrub another toilet," Sasha moaned.

They all laughed.

"You got that right," Mitchell said.

"Well, the way things have been going," Sasha said, "my guess would be they're going to have us use everything we learned today in some form or fashion in the hotel."

"You're probably right," Mitchell said. "That's the way it's been going all along."

"Have any of you noticed that there are equal numbers of women and men?" Misty said.

"Oh no, you're not back to that again are you?" Sasha asked, looking at her friend.

"I'm sure you're trying to make a point," Mitchell said with a half smile.

Misty went on to tell everyone her theory behind the *Heartbreak Hotel* reality TV show. "It all makes perfect sense," she said. "Every reality show, game show, talk show, whatever you want to call them, they're all based on relationships. What would make this program any different from all the others?"

"It would be taking things a bit far, don't you think?" Tina asked.

"Just my thoughts. But I'd bet money that I'm closer to the truth than any of you are willing to admit."

"And what if you are?" Mitchell asked. "How do you see this all playing out?"

"I don't know. But just like all the other reality TV shows, when it gets right down to it, somebody's going to have to make the hard decision."

The waitress appeared and began serving their lunch orders, momentarily quieting any further conversation. For the next ten minutes all that could be heard at the table was the clanking of knives and forks against the plates.

Mitchell finished off the rest of his salmon salad, leaned back in his chair and stretched just a little. "That was excellent," he said. He checked his watch. "We'd better be heading back."

They got up and filed out of the restaurant, heading back over to the lounge.

"You all ready for round two?" Roger asked.

"May the best man win," Mitchell said.

"Don't you mean the best woman?" Sasha and Misty said in unison.

When they returned to the meeting area, all of the judges were already in place. This time it was Brian who took the microphone.

"Welcome back, everyone, and congratulations to all of you who are still part of the competition." He opened the folder, reviewed it and then looked out at the small gathering in front of him. "Based on everything that you learned this morning, what you will be doing for the balance of the afternoon is working within the hotel, assigned to a specific area to carry out specific tasks using all the information that you have gained so far. Of course, you will be supervised, filmed and evaluated." He looked from one face to the other. "What I would like each of you to do, please, is come up and get the envelope here on the table when I call your name."

One by one the final eight contestants went to the table and took the envelope with their name on it then returned to their seats.

"Inside those envelopes are your assignments and the names of your hotel sponsors. That is the person who will answer your questions and provide you with all of the resources you need to complete your task."

Not to be left out, Charlotte took her turn. "This is where things really get tough. You are all on your own. You must use your skills, experience and the knowledge that you gained here in order to win. There is one caveat. You must not, under any circumstances, share with any other contestant what your assignment is. If you do, it is reason for immediate elimination."

"Dang." Misty hissed under her breath.

Sasha nudged her to be quiet.

"So that you all can be prepared for the challenge ahead, you have the night off. I suggest that you review your assignments and get a good night's sleep. You're going to need it." With that she turned and left the room. The other three judges trooped out behind her and the contestants followed suit.

"I'll show you mine if you show me yours," Mitchell whispered in Sasha's ear as they walked toward the outdoor lobby.

She glanced up at him, smiling. "Very funny. But I'm game if you are," she tossed back, her intent as clear as the Caribbean Waters.

"Want to order up some drinks or would you prefer the bar?"

"Let's go to the bar," she said. "It's still so lovely out. We can stroll along the beach for a little while before going up."

"Whatever the lady wants."

They didn't even notice that they'd peeled away from the others without saying good-night until they were seated at the bar.

Sasha looked around. "Where did they go?"

Mitchell shifted around in his seat. "Humph, got me. Maybe they had other plans." He turned back around as the bartender approached.

"What can I do you for tonight?" he asked with a big grin as he wiped down the counter in front of them.

Mitchell turned to Sasha. "What do you have a taste for?"

"Hmmm, how about a berry mimosa."

"No problem. And you, sir?"

"I'll stick with the rum punch."

The bartender went to fix their drinks and Mitchell turned to Sasha. "Isn't that envelope burning your fingers?"

"Of course it is. I'm dying to find out." She drew in a breath, placed the envelope on the counter and her hand on top of it. "But it can wait. Whatever is in there isn't going to change anytime soon."

"True," Mitchell said as the bartender returned with their drinks. He took a sip of his drink and nodded his appreciation to the bartender. "But I was a Boy Scout and part of the Scout Oath is to always be prepared. Can't be prepared if you don't know what you are preparing for."

Sasha grinned. "Oh, any excuse," she said as they both went for their envelopes and opened them simultaneously.

For several moments they were generally quiet except for the murmurs of "hmmm" as they read the contents and sipped their drinks.

Mitchell finished first and slid his papers back in the envelope. Thoughtfully, he finished off his drink while Sasha finished reading.

When she was done she turned halfway in his direction. "Want to take that walk on the beach now?"

"Sure." He dug in his pants pockets for a tip and left it on the counter.

They walked through the bar and dance area and directly out onto the beach.

Mitchell took her hand. Sasha's first instinct was to look around to see who was watching, but the instant her pulse settled she realized it didn't matter. She squeezed his hand.

They walked along the shore, not close enough for their feet to get wet, but enough to feel the spray of the surf.

"Let's head up that way," Mitchell said, pointing to a short bluff of rocks.

Sasha reached down and took off her shoes, tucked her precious envelope under her arm and her shoes in her free hand. "I'd rather have sand in between my toes than caked in my sneakers any day."

"You have a point." Mitchell followed suit and they continued.

They reached the rock formation and Mitchell helped Sasha climb up, then he took a seat beside her. For several moments they took in the magnificence of the scenery in front of them.

The sun barely hovering above the ocean was a brilliant burnt orange, casting beams of light that rippled over the water, bathing the swimmers, the rocky cliffs beyond and the miles of trees and beaches in a shimmering glow of perfection that only nature could create.

"I don't think I could ever get tired of looking at the sunrise and sunset out here," Sasha said softly.

"We certainly don't have anything like this in Georgia."

"That we don't." She drew her knees up to her chest and rested her arms across them. "Why did you really enter this contest?" she asked. "I know it's more than just winning, or getting back what you lost. What's the real reason?"

"As hard as it may be to believe, that is the reason. At least a major part of it. It *is* about getting back what I lost, but not only the physical things—the restaurant, the house—it's…"

"It's what? What do you mean?"

He glanced away. "I can't explain it to you," he said his tone suddenly clipped. How could he possibly explain to this beautiful, talented and accomplished woman that back home he was a failure. People who once called themselves friends refused to return any of his calls. Customers who'd frequented his restaurant quickly passed him on the street with no more than sad smiles. Banks had stopped lending, creditors called nonstop. The circles he once traveled in were broken. He knew all that was part of the reason he'd tried to hold on to Regina. She represented the life he'd built for himself, one of success and achievement, the total opposite of the life he'd grown up living. It was his ambition and desire for a better life that had gotten him a scholarship to college. That was where he'd met Alan Thornton, his best friend. If it hadn't been for him, Mitchell wasn't sure how he would have gotten through the past year.

Sasha watched his profile in the waning light, the hard lines of his jaw, the slope of his nose, the flare of his lips, the curve of his brow. For all the hard angles and masculinity he exuded, she saw and sensed a side of him that he kept hidden, the part of him that felt things beneath the surface. That is the Mitchell Davenport that drew her like a moth to a flame. She knew it was dangerous, but she couldn't seem to tear herself away from the heat that could surely singe her heart for good if she wasn't careful.

He'd given her glimpses when he'd told her about losing his home and business and Regina walking out on him. But it was more what he didn't say that affected her—how those losses, one after another, took a toll on him mentally and emotionally.

She wouldn't push the issue. If things worked out between them, he'd tell her in time. She was certain of that. She leaned closer to him and rested her head on his shoulder.

"I've been dreaming of having something of my own for as long as I can remember," she said softly.

Mitchell relaxed his body and wrapped his arm around Sasha.

"I watched my mother and father build their dream, a dream so big and demanding that there was never room for anyone else's dreams. My sister married a bastard of a man in order to pretend to have a life of her own." She drew in a breath as Mitchell gently ran a hand up and down her arm. "Me…I became the go-to girl, the one the entire family depended on. I'm thirty-two years old and my mother was upset that I was going on vacation, that I was taking time away from the business." She chuckled sadly. "Can you believe that? Don't get me wrong, I love my family dearly. It's just that they are totally draining. If it wasn't for my friend April I would never have gotten up the nerve to enter this competition."

"So, if you win, how do you think your family will handle it?"

"I'm sure my mom will have a fit." She peeked up at him. "Don't tell anyone, but I told my sister, Tristan."

Mitchell chuckled. "I won't tell if you won't tell that I told my best friend, Alan. He drove me to the airport."

They both laughed as they rocked back and forth together, wrapped in an embrace.

So he did have friends, a life, someone who cared about him, Sasha mused, reflecting on the tidbit of information that Mitchell had divulged. She smiled into the darkness.

Chapter 15

It was nearly midnight by the time they returned to the hotel. The corridor on the third floor was empty when Sasha opened her room door and let them in.

For whatever reason she was suddenly nervous, as if this was their first time together, and she made busy work of straightening up and moving things around the room to buy time and clear her head.

She felt him behind her before he touched her. He placed his hand on her shoulder and gently turned her around to face him.

"What is it? You don't have to do this if you don't want to."

"No," she assured him with a swift shake of her head. "That's not it."

"Then what is it?"

She sighed and finally sat down. She glanced sheepishly up at him. "All of a sudden I feel so uncertain, like a teenager on first date."

He sat down beside her. "This *is* a first date. Remember? We're starting over." He smiled gently at her.

She leaned against him. "I don't want this competition to come between us and what we're trying to build. And I don't want what we're trying to build to be overshadowed by sex."

He bit back a smile. "Okay. Understood." He took her hand and pulled her to her feet. "Do you trust me?"

She frowned. "Depends…"

Mitchell laughed. "Come on. I want to engage you in something that I think will help you to realize that for me it's more than sex."

"Where are we going?"

He led her into the bathroom and turned on the shower. "Do you have any candles?"

She blinked in confusion. "No…why?"

"Never mind. Not to worry." He moved toward her. "For this to work, you have to trust me, trust that I won't hurt you, trust that I only want to make you happy."

Her heart thumped as his gaze held hers and he reached for the hem of her top to pull it over her head. His finger reached out and gently stroked the rise of her breasts. He reached for the shirred waistband of her gauzy skirt and wiggled it down her hips until she was standing before him in a ivory-colored bra and thong.

A deep groan rumbled in his chest and he continued to undress her. When he was done, he dimmed the overhead lights and kept on the lights over the sink to achieve the atmosphere he wanted. He scanned the top of the vanity and noticed her bottle of body wash. He held it up with a question in his eyes.

She nodded.

He undressed and kicked his clothes to the side, then took her hand as they stepped into the shower, pulling the clear curtain around them.

"Turn around," he said.

She did as instructed so that her back was facing him. Slowly he began to lather her back, her behind, her thighs and her calves, then he massaged the creamy shower soap into her skin with tender circular strokes. He moved expertly up and down her body, covering every dip and curve until the room was filled with the aromatic scent of her jasmine wash.

Sasha closed her eyes and braced her hands

against the wall as the sensuous massage continued, ebbing and flowing in intensity. She moaned when the pads of his thumbs brushed the undersides of her breasts before he turned her around to face him.

His eyes glowed in the semidarkness, intense and focused only on her. It was heady and thrilling to see that kind of blatant desire and know that it was directed at her. She wanted him to take her right there and then. Whatever he wanted she was willing to give, as long as he would never stop looking at her with that burning hunger in his eyes.

He gave the same intimate care to her front as he did to her back, caressing, massaging, stroking, all without saying a word. He rinsed her off then switched places with her beneath the water, where he quickly soaped, rinsed and got out.

He wrapped her in a towel and, amid squeals of delighted surprise, picked her up and carried her into the bedroom.

Like fine china, he laid her down and removed the towel. For several moments he stood above her, taking her in as if seeing her for the very first time and he was determined to remember every inch of her.

She started to speak.

Mitchell put his finger to his lips and slowly shook his head. He unwrapped the towel that he'd draped around his waist and placed it at the end of the bed.

Sasha drew in a breath. Seeing him fully aroused always took her aback. She knew how threatening he appeared but she also knew the magic he could wield.

He sat down next to her, took two pillows and put them beneath her head. "I want you to be able to see what I'm doing." Then he took another pillow, wrapped it in a towel, and placed it beneath her hips.

"Just relax and breathe," he said gently. Mitchell positioned himself between her slightly parted thighs, then separated them a bit more and pushed her knees up so that her center was open only to him.

He'd noticed a bottle of baby oil in the bathroom and brought it out with them. He poured a quarter-sized amount in his palms and rubbed his hands briskly together until the oil was heated. Then he poured more onto his hands.

Leaning forward he began to massage her breasts with the warm oil in slow, circular motions, cupping them, lifting them, using his palms to rotate around her nipples.

Sasha's breath hitched and escalated as pleasure flowed through her.

"Breathe." He applied more oil to his hands and began working his way down her body in the same, slow motions, covering her skin in the warm oil, his hands sliding along her body like silk.

When he reached her mound, he pressed his

palm firmly against it, then lifted and lowered the base of his palm, teasing her. He poured a small amount of the oil on her so that it dripped between her lower lips. He then gently squeezed the outer lips between his thumb and forefinger then slid the two fingers delicately up and down either side.

Sasha's soft moans filled the air like music, and Mitchell continued to play his masterpiece.

"Take a deep breath," he whispered as he tenderly captured her pulsing bud between his fingers. Her hips rose. Her inner thighs trembled. "Relax, baby. Breathe. Just go with it." With his palm facing upward he gently inserted his finger, moving it in and out in a come-here motion against the spongy wall. Her entire body quivered. A deep moan pushed up from her soul and consumed her.

Sasha felt as if her body were separating from her mind and she was soaring through the hills and valleys of erotic delight. Wave after wave of pleasure flowed through her as Mitchell continued his intimate massage of her body.

For more than an hour, Mitchell paid homage to her body, taking her to heights she'd never before experienced, until she was completely free—mind, body and soul.

Slowly bringing her down from the peak of pleasure, he covered her with a sheet and let her drift off into a deep, satisfied sleep.

When she awoke sometime near dawn, there was a note on the pillow next to her. "Breakfast on the beach. Our spot. I'll bring everything we need. Six-thirty."

Sasha stretched and smiled, her body feeling light and strangely energized. She turned to peek at the digital clock on the nightstand—5:45 a.m.

"Hmmmm," she hummed, stretching some more before getting up. The previous night began taking shape in her head as she floated to the bathroom. Her body still tingled and her mind felt so clear and in tune with every nuance around her.

She'd never before experienced the kind of sensual heights that Mitchell had taken her to last night, all without having sex, at least not in the traditional sense. She'd heard of tantric sex, but she'd always thought it was some mysterious, mystic practice that was more hype than anything else. She could not have been more wrong. One of the items on her self-improvement-list was to learn the techniques herself and start practicing on Mitchell.

After a quick shower, she dressed in an ankle-length skirt in a soft peach color and paired it with a peach and lemon-colored camisole. Stuck her pretty, polished feet into a comfortable pair of espadrilles, grabbed her bag and headed for her rendezvous.

* * *

Mitchell had arrived at six, secured their spot and set out the breakfast. The night he'd spent with Sasha continued to resonate through him, like the sounds of a sweet lullaby. It was the first time he'd explored the art of tantric sex and he was glad that it was with Sasha. He felt a kind of connection with her that he'd never had with anyone else. The experience was beyond physical. It was emotional, taking them to a new level of intimacy.

He spread the blanket and was taking out a flask of coffee when he saw her walking across the beach toward him. For a moment the world stood still and held her in repose. The glow of the rising sun merged with the colors of her outfit giving her an almost iridescent glow.

"Good morning," she said while gathering her skirt around her legs and sitting down on the blanket.

"'Mornin'. Rest well?"

The question held a double meaning that they both understood.

She smiled shyly as memories of the night before flashed in her head. A warm flush tickled her skin. Her gaze rested on his face. "Very," she said softly. "So…what do we have here?"

With a flourish, Mitchell opened the covered trays that he'd secured from the restaurant—with a bit of bribing. Succulent island fruits, cottony-soft eggs, steamed fish and turkey sausage.

"Help yourself," he said, handing her a plate.

Sasha loaded her plate, suddenly ravenous, and they ate in silence under the glow of the morning sun with the soft pounding of the waves against the shore in the background.

"I wonder what they'll have us do today," Sasha said as she sipped her coffee.

"Whatever will work us to the bone, I'm sure."

They laughed.

"Winning is important to you, isn't it?"

Mitchell leaned back on his elbow and looked at her. "Honestly?"

She nodded.

"Yes, it is. For a variety of reasons."

She knew some of the reasons. He'd told her a bit about his business, the loss of it and his home, compounded by his breakup with Regina. What little she knew and understood about men told her they defined their manhood by the things they could acquire, their ability to take care of themselves and their families. Without those things, men sometimes felt insecure. It was one of the reasons why so many families broke up and relationships fell apart.

Her situation was different. Yes, she wanted to win, but for other reasons. She wanted her own destiny. She wanted to disengage herself from the ties that her family had saddled her with all these years. She wanted freedom, to be seen as an individual, not an extension of some ideal.

"We'd better be heading back," Mitchell said, noting the time.

Sasha sat up and helped him return the items to the trays and gather up the utensils.

"I never thanked you for last night," she said quietly as she stood to fold the blanket. She avoided his gaze.

"I hope it was as much your pleasure as it was mine." He grinned.

Sasha flushed. "If you're looking for an answer, it's yes."

"We'll have to try it again sometime."

Sasha's heart thumped with anticipation.

Chapter 16

The group gathered in the lounge area for their assignments. The tension was palpable as they sat around waiting for the judges to appear. The wait wasn't long.

Charlotte, as usual, led the way and stood at the front of the room. She waited for everyone to quiet down.

"Good morning. There are only eight of you left. At the end of this competition there will be two."

A groan flitted around the room.

"Today, you will all be returning to the hotel that you worked on when you arrived. Everything that you learned when you shadowed the Seasons Hotel employees you will now put to work. Your task, along with the other contestants is to get the hotel in shape. That includes ordering food, linens, furniture, accessories, interviewing staff, landscaping, developing promotional material and setting up a billing system in preparation for the guests who will be occupying the hotel at the end of next week."

"Dayum," Misty murmured.

"As you will recall the hotel is two-sided. Half of you will be assigned to one side and the other half the other side. You'll need to pick a team leader for each side who will be responsible for assigning tasks. Any questions?" She looked around the room. "Good," she said when she received none. "Your teams have been preselected. So when your names are called please come forward and stand to my right. The first group will be team A and will be responsible for the west wing of the hotel. Team B will be responsible for the east wing."

Sasha and Misty wound up on the same team again, but they'd lost Tina and gained Joe and Robert. Mitchell and Sasha remained on opposing sides.

"The shuttle is out front to take you all over to the hotel. You will be working until eight tonight when the shuttle will come back to pick you up." She smiled brightly. "Okay, everyone, good luck."

On the ride over, Joe and Robert introduced themselves. Both of them were from New York.

Joe was a former financial advisor and Robert was a short-order cook in a midtown café.

They seemed nice enough, Sasha mused as they talked about their lives in the Big Apple and the circumstances that had brought them to the competition. Both of them had applied on dares from friends. From listening to their reasons for being there, Sasha felt that they were really in it for the publicity, and it wouldn't matter that much to either of them if they didn't win. There was no real sense of desperation or even determination for that matter, both qualities that were needed to be a winner.

Sasha stared out of the window. If she was going to win this thing, she was going to have to work twice as hard. It was apparent from watching Misty flirt that she was more interested in catching a guy than in winning the big prize.

When they pulled up in front of the hotel, it didn't look quite as awful as it had the first day, but it was still in need of major renovation if anyone was to be enticed to stay there.

They all piled out of the van along with the camera crew that was recording their every move.

Brian stood in front of them. "Can I have everyone's attention? I'm sure you are all wondering, or at least you should have been wondering, how you were going to accomplish everything being asked of you." His eyes scrolled the expectant faces. "Each team will be given fifty thousand dollars to pay for your needs. Of course, the team that does the best and spends the least will win the competition."

"Now that's what I'm talking about," Misty said to applause from the group.

"We'll give you ten minutes to decide who will be team captain and then you will get your money voucher."

The two groups broke off to discuss their strengths and weaknesses.

"Since I've been dealing in finances I have no problem handling the budget," Joe said.

"I've worked in a hotel for several years," Sasha piped up. "And if there are no objections, I want to lead the team." She looked from one to the other.

"Fine with me," Misty said.

Joe shrugged.

"I can handle anything having to do with food," Robert said.

"And I'll handle the décor and promotions," Misty offered.

"Then it's settled," Sasha said. "Are we all in agreement?"

Everyone nodded.

Sasha drew in a breath and walked over to Brian at the same moment that Mitchell did. They looked at each other.

"I guess you two are the team leaders," Brian said, taking two envelopes out of his pocket and handing one to Sasha and the other to Mitchell. "Good luck." He turned and walked back to the shuttle.

"Guess this is it," Mitchell said.

"Yeah, it is."

"Good luck," he said sincerely.

"You, too."

They separated and the competition began in earnest.

When they entered the hotel they were thrilled to find working phones as well as brand-new computers complete with Internet service.

Each team ventured off to its respective side of the hotel.

"Okay, first things first, we have to get a list of everything we need to get done, and who is going to be responsible for carrying out the tasks," Sasha said, easily stepping into her role as leader.

They huddled around the front desk and began making a list for day one. It began with ordering supplies for the bedrooms and the kitchen. That task was given to Misty. Robert took over figuring out what staff they would need and Joe said he would set up a billing and reservation system on the computer and maintain a running list of their expenditures.

With the tasks assigned, Sasha worked on what special amenities would be offered to their guests as well as planning the menu with Joe's help. She also took on the responsibility of decorating the reception area, the restaurant and bar, the bedrooms, hallways and the pool area. It was going to be a grueling, non-stop week, but Sasha was up to the task. She was high on adrenaline and expectation. She knew she could do this. Her vision for the hotel wing was a practice run for her dream resort. Owning and operating a resort of her very own was less than two weeks away. She could feel it in her gut.

The better part of the morning was used to place phone calls to local vendors who supplied all of the hotels on the island and negotiating the best deals. Sasha took a trip into St. John's and began purchasing some of the items that she needed to give the hotel the ambiance she envisioned. She returned to several of the local shops that she and Mitchell had visited when he gave her the grand tour. She had a momentary twinge of guilt that she was using their time together to work against him. But all's fair in love and war, she reminded herself, confident that Mitchell would use all of his know-how and resources as well.

And he was. His expertise in running his own restaurant, from staffing to billing to menus and guest relations came in handy. He doled out assignments to his teammates with a vision of creating Davenport's with an island flair. He not only *wanted* to win this competition, he *needed* to win it. He needed to show all those fair-weather friends that he wasn't a failure, that he wasn't some poor guy who'd fallen on hard times, that he would never give up.

Sure for a while, he'd given up on himself. It happens when everything that makes you who you are is suddenly taken away from you, leaving you naked for all the world to see. Only those who have experienced it can understand what it feels like to go from having your own home to losing it, from having your own business to working day jobs just to put food in your mouth and a roof over your head. Only then can you understand the humiliation when all those who you thought were in your corner barely look you in the eye. Had it not been for Alan, his one friend, he wasn't sure where he would be today.

He looked around at the magnitude of what needed to be accomplished in such a short span of time and was energized. This was his for the taking. He'd show them all.

The next few days it was non-stop traffic in and out of the hotel. Deliveries arrived every hour from all over the island—furniture, silverware, linens, pillows, towels, pots and pans, couches and curtains.

Both teams eyed each and every delivery trying to gain some insight on what the other team was doing and how they were pulling it all together. No one was giving up any secrets.

At night, too exhausted to do more than share a look, Sasha and Mitchell retired to their separate rooms, pushing aside their longing for each other in lieu of the prize of a lifetime. After this was all over and the competition was behind them, they individually vowed, they would pick up where they'd left off. Until then, there could only be one objective. But their pent-up desires, the unrelenting temptation of seeing each other every day and not being able to touch, to laugh, to be privately in each other's presence got the better of them.

Midway through the week, after returning from an unusually humid day filled with lifting and storing and endless deliveries, Sasha and Mitchell found themselves alone on the elevator.

"How have you been?" Mitchell began, leaning across Sasha and intentionally brushing his arm against her breast as he pressed the button for the third floor.

Air hissed between Sasha's teeth at the brief but tantalizing contact. "Fine. Better than I expected."

He turned, leaned casually up against the elevator wall and looked her over from head to toe. "I miss you. The hell with protocol, being tired and this damned competition. I want you." He crossed the short space, his hands pressed against the wall on either side of her and he was inches from kissing her when the door opened.

Sasha barely heard the laughter of the couple boarding the elevator over the thundering beat of her heart. The door closed and they rode one more flight. The instant they stepped off they burst into laughter at being so horny and nearly getting caught.

"This is bad," Sasha giggled.

"Haven't come that close to getting busted since my college days."

Sasha slowly sobered as they walked down the corridor in the direction of her room. She swallowed. "What college did you attend?"

"Morehouse." The pride was evident in his voice.

She glanced up at him. "A Morehouse man."

"Through and through."

"It's definitely one of the things that I missed, going away to college. Or just the experience of attending an historically black college. I think if you have the chance and the money it's the thing to do. I know I'd want that for my kids."

"Kids, as in plural?"

She shrugged slightly. "At least two. You can't call yourself a real parent until you have more than one."

His dark eyes sparkled with curiosity. "And why is that?"

"Well," she said in all sincerity, "with one child you always know who's to blame."

He looked at her for a moment, then tossed his head back and laughed. "You know something, you're absolutely right."

They stopped in front of her door. She turned to him with her back against it. "What about you?"

He angled his head to the side.

"Kids. Do you want any?"

He lowered his gaze a moment before looking directly into her eyes. "With the right woman."

Heat flooded her face from the intensity of the look he gave her. It was as if he were seeing *into* her, exploring not what was visible on the outside but the secrets, the dreams, the desires that she held in her soul. It was a mental undressing that left her shaky and wet with longing. She gripped the handle of the door, just as Mitchell blocked out the world with a searing kiss.

A helpless groan rose from the depths of his throat when the sweetness of her tongue played with his. His arm snaked around her waist, pulling her flush and tight up against him, sealing her body with his.

This is so crazy, he thought as he kissed, held and stroked this perfect work of art in his arms. Sasha was making him crazy. Every time he saw her he wanted to stop what he was doing and be with her. As much as he'd thought that Regina was the one for him, he'd never felt the kind of intensity with Regina that he did with Sasha. Being with her made him want to be the very best man he could be. She listened, she laughed, she offered her opinion without forcing it on him. She had goals and dreams that didn't hinge on anyone else's efforts but her own. He admired that in her. And she was sexy as hell. God, he couldn't get enough of her. Whenever he thought he was drained of loving, there was still more to give— and he wanted to be sure that Sasha was the one he was giving it to.

He took her hand and pressed it against the hard rise in his pants. "Feel that," he ground out against her mouth. "That's only half as much as I want you." He took a reluctant step back.

Sasha watched him. The burning hunger in his eyes was frightening in its desire for her, but what was more terrifying was her equal hunger for him.

What constantly sparked between them was an ongoing inferno that could be tempered but never fully extinguished.

"Come inside," she said on a hot breath of desire. She fumbled in her purse for her key card and opened the door.

The instant they were inside they began disrobing, tossing garments to the floor in their haste to claim each other once again.

Sasha would never tire of looking at Mitchell's naked body. He was a work of art. The smooth chocolate skin layered over hard, rippling muscle was the ultimate turn-on. The curve of his jaw, the slope of his dark, deep-set eyes beneath thick lashes and thicker brows easily reminded her of the model Tyson Beckford.

Their loving was smooth, flowing like the gentle waves of the Caribbean, building in intensity, cresting and falling and cresting again as they clung to each other, undulating with the tide.

Yet, even as they spoke in the hushed whispers of lovers, spurring each other on, they both understood that this magic that they shared could end up tossing them alone against the shore.

"I'm going to head back to my room," Mitchell said against the curve of her neck.

She snuggled closer. "Do you have to go?"

"I don't want to, but I'd better." He kissed her cheek and brushed the loose hair away from her face.

She sighed heavily. "I wish things were different," she confessed.

He rose up on his elbow and looked at her. "What do you mean?"

"I wish that we weren't on opposite sides. That we weren't competing for the same thing. That it wouldn't interfere with what we have going on."

Mitchell sat up and put his feet on the floor. "Unfortunately, that's not the case," he said in a short tone that sparked Sasha's radar. She sat up as well.

"One of us is going to win this competition," she said. "What then?"

He stood. "I guess we'll have to work that out when the time comes." He reached for his shorts and put them on, keeping his back to her.

A tightness grew in her stomach. She didn't like what she was feeling or Mitchell's almost indifferent reaction. "I guess we will," she tossed back with the same cavalier tone.

He stole a quick glance at her over his shoulder then finished dressing. She watched him in silence.

"Good luck tomorrow," he said before walking out the door.

The gentle click of the door closing sounded like shotgun fire in Sasha's chest. She pulled the sheet up to her chin and stared out at the cloudless sky beyond her terrace window.

Chapter 17

As much as she wanted to do otherwise, she could not focus her attention on Mitchell and what might or might not be. Every ounce of energy and creativity was needed to pull off one of the toughest jobs of her life. Her days were filled with organizing, planning, instructing, supervising her team, overseeing that the shipments were correct, arguing with vendors and trying to remain positive as the clock continued to click toward the last days of the competition.

"Do you think we're going to have it together in time?" Misty asked her as they directed one of the delivery men to the kitchen area.

"We have no choice. We have to finish." Sasha took a breath and looked around. "We've done an incredible job, no matter what happens," she said, turning a soft and thankful smile on Misty.

"This has been your baby from the beginning," Misty said. "It's your vision. And I gotta admit, I'm impressed. I know I could not have done it."

Sasha draped her arm around Misty's tired shoulders. "It was a group effort."

"That may be true, but the group can't win." Misty gave Sasha a look she couldn't quite place before walking away.

Since that last night they were together, Sasha and Mitchell had managed to stay away from each other—whether it was intentional or circumstantial, Sasha couldn't be sure. What she was certain of was that she missed him—terribly. During the day, her time and mind were occupied with getting the hotel ready for guests. But at night, the hours dragged, and her body and her heart ached for his touch.

It had only been a matter of weeks since they'd first met, but in that short span of time her feelings for him had grown and blossomed, consuming her. There were times during the early-morning hours just before dawn when she was willing to give it all up if she could be assured that they would be together. But she knew better. Giving up on her dream for a possibility was not why she'd come. Yet, as the days continued to mount, she began to question what was really important.

The hotel's opening day had finally arrived and all of the contestants were called into the lobby of the renovated hotel for a final meeting.

"All of you have done a phenomenal job," Charlotte began. "This evening, you will check in your first guests who will remain with us for the weekend. It's clear that each wing has its own signature style, which is what the judges and your guests will be looking for." She checked her watch. "The first guests will be arriving in about an hour, so now is the time for a last-minute sweep of the accommodations and to go over with your staff what is expected of them during the weekend. Best of luck to both teams. Oh, one last thing." She smiled slowly. "I may have neglected to mention this, but your guests will only be staying on your side of the hotel for one night. In the morning they will check out and move to the other side of the hotel." She turned and walked away. The cameras were trained on the contestant's faces to catch every expression.

"Any more bombshells?" Sasha said under her breath.

"So instead of having the entire weekend to win the guests over we have a day and a night," Joe said.

"Looks that way," Sasha said. "And it's going to be the best one-night stay they've ever experienced. Come on, let's get busy."

By noon, all twelve of Sasha's guests had arrived—four singles and four couples. Sasha, remembering the confused looks on arriving guests' faces at the registration counter at the Summit, had hired two beautiful high-school girls to serve as official greeters, handing incoming guests a brochure of the facility, answering questions, offering them free refreshments in the lobby and securing a bellhop to assist with their luggage.

Each of the guests were offered several resort packages to choose from that included in-room massages, spa treatments, an in-room trainer, and twenty-four-hour bar service among several other amenities, one of which was a health-food menu that was Sasha's pride and joy.

The rooms were designed around the ancient Chinese design principles of feng shui. There were soft pastels on the walls and bolder accents for the bed comforters and sheets. There were no mirrors in the bedroom since with feng shui they were believed to disturb sleep. Guests could choose soothing music that was piped in through speakers when the lights were turned off for sleep. The rooms exuded a feeling of tranquility from the moment you walked in. Each of the guests in Sasha's wing commented on how peaceful they felt.

"Looks like we're off to a great start," Sasha said to Misty as they headed to the kitchen to check on the food preparation.

"If the menu is a hit—like I know it will be—it's gonna take a miracle to for the other team to beat us."

The rest of the day into the evening until check-out time next morning went without a hitch. The guests were pampered, and, as anticipated, they loved the healthy-diet menu and the array of special amenities that were offered.

Sunday afternoon arrived too soon and the final decision was upon them.

"All of the guests had an opportunity to spend time in both wings," Brian said. "Comment cards were provided and each of the services was given points. We will be going over the answers from the guests and reviewing the tapes. The shuttle bus is outside ready to take you all back to your hotel. Everyone is expected to meet in the lounge tomorrow morning at nine when we will announce the winners of the competition. Get some sleep and we'll see you all tomorrow."

Sasha spent a fitful night. She went over everything her team had done, looking for any shortcomings, something she could have done differently or better. She couldn't come up with anything. She flipped onto her side and drew her knees close to her chest. Had Mitchell's team done better? She had no idea what he'd done since neither team had been allowed to venture outside of their wing. It was up to the judges now. She'd done all she could. It was out of her hands.

The following morning, Sasha was up before the sun. She dressed and decided to take a walk along the beach before the day began. As she strolled along the shore with the cool waters washing over her bare feet, she noticed the silhouette perched atop the cluster of rocks where she and Mitchell had shared breakfast at sunrise. Drawing closer, she saw movement and her heart beat faster in her chest. It was Mitchell. She'd know him anywhere. The distinct outline of his body was etched in her memory. But it was more than the physical aspects of him. There was a connection between them that went beyond the superficial, some inexplicable link that bound them.

They hadn't spoken since the morning he'd left her room, and she'd tried, through work and focusing on the tasks at hand, to block him out of her mind. As much as she didn't want to accept it, the very thing that had brought them together had pulled them apart. No matter what happened at this point, she knew things could never be what she'd hoped for, and she'd been naive to think otherwise. It was clear from his actions what was important, and she couldn't blame him. They each had an agenda. And they'd momentarily allowed their feelings to get in the way. Falling in love with Mitchell Davenport was not part of her plan.

She hadn't said the words out loud. She hadn't admitted it to anyone, not even April, but she'd fallen in love with him, as ridiculous as that was. Had anyone else told her that, she would say they were crazy, that they'd confused good old-fashioned sex with love.

But she hadn't confused them, and that was what was so painful. It was what kept her up at night and made her rethink what she was doing and what was important. It was what filled her mind and her heart whenever she thought of him, saw him or heard his voice. He was who she wanted. But the reality was she could not have both him and her dream, and it was tearing her up inside.

Before he saw her, she turned and began heading back to her room.

Mitchell watched her leave. He started to call out to her, but thought better of it. What could he say to her? What could he do to change the awkward circumstance he'd found himself in? When he'd decided to come to Antigua and take a chance on changing his life, it hadn't included finding and falling for Sasha. But he had. As much as he'd tried to block her from his mind, he couldn't. She was in his blood.

He'd come out here to what they'd dubbed "their place" to think, and he'd come to a decision.

Chapter 18

When the two teams gathered in the lounge they were informed that they would be moving to the main ballroom of the hotel. When the doors to the ballroom opened they were stunned to find that it had been set up for a live television feed, complete with a studio audience, cameras, blinding stage lights, a dais for the contestants and the panel of judges waiting to cast their votes.

When the contestants entered, the room broke out in thunderous applause. Many of the audience members were calling them by name.

"What the hell is going on?" Sasha mouthed to

Misty as they were ushered toward their seats. "How do they know who we are?"

"We love you, Sasha!"

"Mitchell is the man. Woo-woo!!"

"Misty, Misty, over here…"

"Go, Joe! Go, Joe…"

"Got me. But this whole experience has been one surprise after another. Maybe this is the latest challenge."

A young blond woman, dressed to the nines in a navy-blue business suit, was apparently the hostess who guided them to their seats then stepped up to the microphone.

"Welcome everyone to *Heartbreak Hotel!* I'm Jessica Lennox."

The crowd roared.

"Tonight is the night we have been watching and waiting for for weeks." She turned and gave an earnest look at the contestants, who remained clueless about what was going on. "Do you think I should let them in on our little secret?" she asked the audience to an ear-splitting response of "Yes." She turned her sky-blue eyes on the perplexed faces of the eight remaining contestants. "Little did you all know that not only was your entire experience here on Antigua taped for television, it was being broadcast across the island every night at nine."

Sasha's hand flew to her mouth in alarm. "Oh my goodness. They didn't."

"And every night the audience voted on who was to stay and who was to go. Tonight we have those figures."

"I'm starting to feel ill," Tina whispered.

"Let's watch some clips," Jessica said.

The audience was entertained with footage of the ten original contestants upon their arrival, their first day of renovating the hotel, right up to opening day when the first guests arrived. But one thing seemed obvious: the cameramen appeared to have been determined to capture every look, conversation, touch or connection that had happened between Mitchell and Sasha. There were shots of them at the bar, walking through the lobby together, along the resort pathways, even one taken the morning they had shared breakfast on the beach.

Sasha wanted to get up, run out and never come back. She was mortified.

Mercifully the lights came up, and the audience broke out into spontaneous applause.

"And we have another surprise for our contestants, don't we, Jessica?" Charlotte said from the judges' table.

"We certainly do."

"What now, the guillotine?" Sasha groaned, silently praying for a natural disaster.

"Everyone except two lucky contestants are in on this surprise," Jessica said. She paused for dramatic effect. The eight contestants eyed each other and one by one they rose to stand beside Jessica until the two remaining contestants seated beneath the hot lights were Sasha and Mitchell.

The audience roared their approval while Sasha and Mitchell stared at each other in utter confusion.

Jessica turned to the perplexed couple with a smile beaming on her peaches-and-cream face. "Mitchell Davenport and Sasha Carrington are *Heartbreak Hotel*'s finalists!"

Her announcement was followed by more cheers and applause. "The goal of this competition was to find someone capable and deserving of running their own hotel or resort. But there is a reason why we named this competition *Heartbreak Hotel*. Our judges and audience members have been watching you both from the beginning and saw the sparks." She grinned. "And the unanimous consensus is that you're perfect for each other." The audience whooped and hollered. "However," she continued, talking over the noise until the crowd quieted, "you both came here for a reason, and that was to win. But in order to win, you have to choose."

She took a sealed envelope from the judges' table and opened it, pulling out a sheet of paper.

"After tallying up all the scores, and including the feedback from the audience and the guests at the hotel—the winner by only two hundred points is…"

From somewhere in the room there was an actual drum roll.

"Sasha Carrington!"

The room exploded in a cacophony of noise.

Sasha screamed. "Oh my God. Oh my God!" Tears of relief and joy sprang from her eyes. Her gaze darted to Mitchell who nodded. "Congratulations," he mouthed.

Jessica held up her hands to quiet the crowd. "There's one more thing," she shouted. "The final step is up to you, Sasha."

Sasha sniffed and wiped her tears. "What do you mean?" she asked, her voice wobbly with emotion.

"You have a decision to make. You can walk away with the hotel and everything that you will need to get started. Or…you can go home with Mitchell Davenport and one million dollars."

Sasha's mouth dropped open as her heart lurched in her chest. Her eyes widened and focused on Mitchell, who was as stunned as she was.

"You have twenty-four hours to make your decision." Jessica turned to face the audience. "What will she choose? The man and the million or the prize of a lifetime, her very own hotel or resort anywhere in the world? Join us tomorrow night for Sasha's decision. I'm Jessica Lennox for *Heartbreak Hotel!* Good night."

The lights dimmed and the audience was guided out of the room by security.

Tina and Misty came running over to where Sasha was still pinned to her seat.

"Congratulations, girl," Misty chirped, squeezing Sasha in a tight hug.

Sasha was still too stunned to respond. Finally she focused on the two conspirators. "You both were in on this?"

They nodded in unison.

"Joe and Richard, too?"

They nodded again.

Sasha drew in a tight breath, pushed back from her seat and stood. Without a word she stormed out, not bothering to look back.

This was not what he'd signed on for, Mitchell thought as he walked along the hotel property. He wasn't upset that he hadn't won outright. He was upset that he'd been set up and now his future rested in Sasha's hands, a tenuous situation for her. But maybe it wasn't.

In the weeks that they'd gotten to know each other, what he'd discovered about Sasha was that she had a single-minded focus. She was the one who had wanted to put a halt to things between them if it meant jeopardizing her chances. But he'd backed her into relenting because of his own burning ambition.

He hadn't come to Antigua to find love, but he had. And because of that he couldn't put Sasha in a position of choosing. It might be egotistical of him to think that she would choose him over her dream, and it was his ego and his feelings for her that would not allow either of them to be put in that position.

Sasha wandered out to the pool behind the main building and was relieved to find herself alone. She found one of the lounge chairs tucked away and out of sight of passersby and curled up on it. How could she possibly choose between her dream and Mitchell? During the weeks that they'd been together he too had become part of her dream.

She'd expected a lot of things from this competition but this last curve ball was not one of them. How could the judges think that this was entertainment—playing havoc with people's lives and emotions? She supposed that was the obsession with reality television—the desire to see other people's struggles, whether physical or emotional. Like witnessing an accident—simply too terrible to look away.

Heartbreak Hotel, she thought morosely. The

game certainly fit the title because she was sure her heart was breaking.

At first Mitchell wasn't sure if he was hearing things or if what he heard was actually someone softly crying. He stepped closer to the wall that separated the pool from the equipment room. Someone *was* crying. He felt guilty, like a voyeur witnessing someone else's pain. He started to walk away but stopped short when he heard Sasha's voice. She was talking with someone and although he couldn't make out all the words, the hurt was evident in her voice. Had something happened back home? He stepped forward with the intention of going to comfort her when he heard his name.

"I don't know what to do, April. This is tearing me apart. I know how much Mitchell wanted this, but…"

He squeezed his eyes shut and lifted his head toward the starry cloudless sky as his gut tightened like a fist. Then he turned and walked away, not wanting to hear any more. He'd been rejected once. He wouldn't wait around for it to happen again.

"What does your heart tell you to do?" April was asking.

"It says to take Mitchell and the money and make a life for both of us. But Mitchell is a proud man. He'd never want to live off of me. He came here to get a new start, rebuild his life. Have something to call his own." A sob caught in Sasha's throat.

"I wish I had a simple answer for you, but I don't. The only thing I can suggest is to talk to him. Tell him how you feel."

Sasha wiped her eyes with the back of her hand. "I'll think about it."

"You don't have much time from what you've told me."

"I know. I know. But I need to think this through."

"Okay, I'm here if you need to talk."

"Thanks."

Sasha disconnected the call and tucked the phone back in her purse. Breathing deeply, she leaned back against the chair and closed her eyes.

Sasha lost count of how many times she'd gotten out of bed during the course of the night to pace the floor and walk out onto the terrace in hopes of being soothed by the gentle lapping of the ocean. Never in her life had she been so conflicted. And she knew that a great deal of her angst was due to how she felt about Mitchell. As hard as it was for her to verbalize and accept it, she'd fallen in love with him, and the very last thing she wanted to do was hurt him.

She was at a crossroads. To take the hotel would be a direct slap in the face to Mitchell. That much she understood, but she also understood that to accept the money and Mitchell would not work either. How could it? That wasn't the kind of man that Mitchell Davenport was. He might have fallen on hard times, but his dignity was intact.

Tell him how you feel. April's words kept playing over and over in Sasha's head. Her temples throbbed from lack of sleep, but she couldn't stay put any longer. She checked the time. Six-thirty. *Our time,* she thought with a pang.

She threw some water on her face, brushed her teeth, pulled on a lightweight jogging outfit and went down the hall his room.

For several moments she stood in front of his door. She couldn't seem to get her hand to knock. She looked left and right along the long corridor. Finally she knocked and waited. Her heart raced so fast she was certain she was going to pass out. The heat of anxiety flooded her body and pounded in her head.

She frowned. No answer. She knocked again. A little harder this time. She waited. Still no answer. She tried one more time before accepting the notion that he was either sleeping like a baby or had gone for his routine walk along the beach.

She started to return to her room, but knew that if she did, she'd lose the nerve that she'd worked up throughout the night. She went in search of Mitchell.

For the next hour, even as the resort began to come to life with guests heading to the beach and breakfast, Sasha continued to look for Mitchell— on the beach, in the restaurant, near the pool, in the exercise room, the lounge, the business office, the lobby. She even returned to his room, thinking that she might have missed him, but even as she did, a dark feeling began to build in her center.

By 8:00 a.m., she'd covered every inch of the hotel property. On her way back to her room she did what she'd been holding off from doing; she stopped at the reception desk.

"Good morning. How can I help you?" the receptionist asked.

"Um, I was looking for one of the guests. Would it be possible for you to ring their room?" She laughed nervously. "We were supposed to meet for breakfast."

"Of course. What is the name of the guest?"

"Mitchell Davenport."

The woman hit a few keys on the computer, frowned and typed some more. She looked up at Sasha. "How do you spell the last name, ma'am?"

Sasha's pulse pounded in her veins. She spelled Mitchell's last name.

The receptionist pressed her lips together as she studied the screen, then she focused on Sasha.

"I'm sorry, but it looks like Mr. Davenport checked out early this morning."

Sasha was too stunned to react.

"Is there anything else I can help you with this morning?"

Sasha blinked, bringing the young woman into focus. She swallowed over the dry knot in her throat. "Uh, no. Thank you very much." She forced a fake smile, turned and walked away, hurrying back to her room, with her gaze trained on the ground so that no one would see her tears.

Chapter 19

"Hey, sis," Sasha said as she lay on her bed, curled up the way she'd done when she was a little girl.

"Sasha!" Tristan said. "How are you? What's going on? And why do you sound like someone just stuck a pin in your balloon?"

Sasha sniffed. "I don't know where to start." She blew out a breath. "Last night…" She paused, trying to get her thoughts together. "Let me begin by saying that the judges pulled several fast ones on us."

"Say what?"

"Yeah, girl." She slowly began filling her sister

in on what had taken place the night before and how awful she had felt after it was all said and done.

"But you won. Simple as that. You worked your butt off. I know you did because that's just how you are. So what are you so upset about? You won! I am so proud of you. Oh, my goodness."

"Hold on, there's more." She told Tristan about the final twist that the judges had thrown in.

"Ohhh, damn."

They were both silent for a moment, their thoughts racing.

"Humph, so what are you going to do?"

"I thought I had it figured out. I was going to go to him and tell him how I felt…"

"And?"

"He's checked out."

"Oh, wow. When?"

"Sometime this morning. While I was pacing the floor he was checking out."

"I'm sorry, sis. Really, I am."

"Yeah."

"Listen, you went there for a reason. You worked hard for it and you won. That's nothing to be ashamed of. The fact that you met someone you could really care about doesn't change that. And if he cares anything about you, he'd want you to follow your dream, Sasha."

Sasha's voice wobbled as her eyes clouded

with tears. "Why did he leave, Tris, without even saying goodbye?"

"Sometimes goodbyes are just too hard."

"Welcome to the finale of *Heartbreak Hotel*," Jessica Lennox announced to the cameras and the live audience. "As you know, last night, Sasha Carrington, our winner had a major decision to make. She had to choose between potential love and potential profit." She turned to Sasha. "Sasha, will you join me at center stage?"

Sasha got up from her stool beside her former teammates and walked to the center of the makeshift stage. Jessica put her arm around Sasha's shoulders.

"Excited?" She beamed as if this was the greatest thing since a Dolce and Gabbana sale.

Sasha, knowing that her every nuance was being taped and ultimately broadcast for the entire world to see, put her best customer-relations smile on her face. "Yes, I am."

"Great. Well look right into that camera and tell the world what your decision is. The man and the million or your very own resort/hotel in Savannah, Arizona, San Francisco or right here in Antigua!"

Sasha blinked several times, drew her shoulders back and looked into the camera.

"This was not an easy decision, no matter what people may think. I truly struggled with what to do, how it would be perceived and what both Mitchell and I came to Antigua to accomplish." She paused a moment. "I decided to take the hotel."

Pounds of confetti and hundreds of balloons in brilliant colors fell from the ceiling to the delight of the studio audience. The excitement and frivolity was the perfect camouflage for the heaviness that weighed down her spirit.

Before she could board her plane back to Savannah, Sasha spent the next day signing documents, having accounts established and going over virtual tours of potential buildings in Savannah for her new business. She felt as if she was walking through a dream. It was all so surreal. Many times she had to pinch herself or take a long look in the mirror to convince herself that it was all real.

The hardest part came the night before she was scheduled to leave. Her heart ached so desperately that she was convinced that hearts really did break. As she walked along the sandy beach, she replayed all the times she and Mitchell had shared together, from the electric moment when they met to the night he introduced her to tantric sex, right up to hearing the words from the receptionist that he was gone.

Would she ever see him again? Did he think about her at all? After a month would any of this even matter?

She wrapped her arms around her waist and gazed out onto the brilliant orange-and-gold horizon. She was going to be fine. She had to be. That's all there was to it. And as the saying went, *this too shall pass.*

Returning to his very small one-bedroom apartment in downtown Atlanta was not only a shock to Mitchell's eyes but a shock to his body. Life in the tropics definitely had its appeal, Mitchell mused—warm sea breezes, beautiful beaches, gorgeous vistas and a kind of social tranquility that was good for the soul. No one was in a hurry. The hustle and bustle was driven by tourists, not the native islanders.

Mitchell put his carry-on in the corner of his bedroom and pulled the second bag behind him. He set that one near the closet. Sitting on the side of the bed he took in his surroundings. Was it possible that his apartment had gotten smaller in the weeks that he'd been gone? He chuckled at the absurdity.

He'd brought in the mail when he came in and began to go through it. Nothing but advertisements and bills. He tossed them aside and flopped back on the bed, tucking his hands behind his head. This wasn't how he'd expected to feel coming home from Antigua. He'd known he'd be elated, on the road to a new life, a brand-new beginning.

None of that had happened, and coming close was worse than losing by a mile.

Yet he knew that wasn't the true source of his mood. As hard as he tried, he couldn't get Sasha off his mind. Checking out of the hotel without seeing her was one of the hardest things he'd had to do since he'd entered the competition. The hellacious weeks that the contestants had been put through were nothing compared to how he'd felt when he saw the hotel get smaller and smaller through the van's window as it rattled down the road.

She probably thought he was a real jerk and a sore loser whose ego had got kicked to the curb. The sad part was he'd never get to tell her otherwise. And it was best this way. He didn't want her thinking that he was hanging around in the hopes of riding her winning coattails. That wasn't the kind of man he was. He was old-school. He lived by the mantra that a man protects, professes and provides. And when he can't do that, he's not a man. As things stood right now, all he could do was profess his feelings for her and that was not enough. So, there was no point in trying to pursue something that could not happen. By the time he got his life in order, Sasha would certainly have found someone who could live up to the expectations of what a man was supposed to be.

In the meantime, he needed to call Alan and let

him know he was back. Maybe they could get together for dinner or a drink. He sat up. Who he really needed to call was his boss over at the bar and make sure he still had a job.

He reached for his cell phone and dialed Harry's Bar and Grill.

"Hey sugah," Vikki, one of the hostesses, said when he identified himself. "When the hell are you coming back? Harry is trying to kill me in here." She laughed good-naturedly.

"That's what I was calling to find out. He around?"

"Yeah, hang on. You still handsome?" she asked in that smoky voice of hers.

"Always to you, Vic."

He could hear her laughing in the background. Several moments later Harry got on the phone and wasted no time in telling him to get in there for the night shift.

"See you at seven, Harry." Mitchell chuckled to himself as he disconnected the call. At least some things didn't change. Guess dinner and drinks with Alan was out. He checked the time. It was barely noon. He took a chance and called Alan at his office at the radio station.

"WVEE, V103," the singsong voice answered.

"Alan Thornton, please."

"Who's calling?"

"Mitchell Davenport."

"Please hold."

Several moments passed before Alan's deep baritone came on the line. With his voice, he should have been one of those "quiet-storm" or "after-dark" DJs, but he'd chose to be behind the scenes in production.

"Hey, man. You home?"

"Just got in."

"Cool. Let's hook up after I get off."

"Can't. Gotta work tonight."

"So I'll stop by Harry's, say around nine."

"See you then."

With that out of the way, Mitchell decided he might as well tackle unpacking his bags and piling up his laundry. If he went to the Laundromat up the street early he could beat the after-work crowd and the college kids that poured in after classes.

With a duffel bag draped over his shoulder and a bottle of detergent in his free hand, Mitchell headed out to the laundry.

As he'd hoped, it was relatively empty, and he'd begun unloading his clothes when he felt a presence next to him. He angled his head to the side to see a very cute young woman in a midriff top that showed off great abs peeking at him. She blushed when he caught her staring.

"Uh, sorry." She smiled meekly. "I know you must have heard this a dozen times, but are you the guy from that new reality show *Heartbreak Hotel?*"

He jerked up so fast he saw spots for a minute. "Huh?"

"I'm sorry. Forget it." She continued putting her clothes in the machine.

Mitchell stood immobile for a minute. How would anyone know about the show? It hadn't aired yet. Had it?

"Excuse me."

The young woman turned to look at him.

"You said *Heartbreak Hotel,* right?"

She nodded. "Yes."

"Has it aired yet?"

"No. But they've been promoting it like crazy for weeks. And you just really look like one of the contestants."

He half grinned. "You know, they say we all have a twin."

"Yeah." She shut the door to the machine, put in her quarters and detergent and walked away.

Mitchell leaned against his machine, watching the woman leave and wondered what was going on.

When he got back home and checked his messages, the last call he expected to receive was one from the television station wanting to do an interview on the local morning show. The caller was from the production department and left a call-back number. Mitchell played the message three times. This was crazy. Can they do this? He went in search of his contract.

By the time he'd scrutinized the fine print, he was convinced that the producers of *Heartbreak Hotel* had the right to pimp him out in order to promote the show. His name and likeness was theirs to use for any promotional purposes related to the show and he could not give away the ending or say anything disparaging about the show, its producers or sponsors.

The gift that doesn't stop giving, he thought, trying to temper his annoyance. He had no one to blame but himself. It wasn't as if he hadn't read the contract before he signed, he simply hadn't thought much would come of the fine print, or, if it did, it would be a result of him winning. He tossed the contract on top of his dresser and figured the folks at *Live in the Morning* could wait a few hours for his response.

Although Harry's was within walking distance of his apartment building he knew he'd be too tired for the walk home when he got off at 1:00 a.m. He went around the back of the building and cranked up his car. It had been a minor blessing that he didn't have a car loan when his finances went belly-up. His midnight-blue Volvo convertible was his pride and joy. A symbol of better days.

In less than five minutes Mitchell was pulling up behind Harry's and parking his car. When he pushed through the wood-and-glass door he was pleasantly surprised to actually feel good about being back. The sense of the familiar, from the sights, sounds and smells to the regulars sitting at the bar, had a calming effect on him.

Vikki tossed her honey-blond weave over her shoulder and beamed at Mitchell when he strolled through the door. She came from behind the counter, draped her arms on either side of his neck and kissed him on the lips. Her eyes, the color of her hair, rolled lustily over him from head to toe.

"You sure look good, baby," she said, rocking her hips from side to side discreetly enough that there was no direct body contact.

Mitchell tapped her lightly on the side of her hip. "So you keep telling me, Vic," he said, extricating himself from her. If he was a different kind of man he would have taken Vikki up on her numerous offers of casual sex. She wasn't bad-looking. She was funny, though maybe not the brightest bulb. But she wasn't his type. *Sasha was.* The thought popped up in his head like a jack-in-the-box, sudden and startling. He shook the idea away. "Where's Harry?"

"In the back," Vikki said, chewing on a wad of spearmint gum. "He's waiting for you."

"Thanks."

"Good to have you back," she called out as he walked around the bar to the office.

He acknowledged her welcome with a wave. He walked down the tight, narrow hallway to the door at the end. He knocked twice.

"Yeah, yeah, come in."

Mitchell stepped into a cloud of cigar smoke. Harry was a mass of contradictions. He had the looks of a young Paul Newman, with the ocean-blue eyes, the voice of Vito Corleone from *The Godfather,* and the disposition of a used-car salesman, always looking for an inside track. Overall, Harry Webb was a pussycat.

He looked at Mitchell through the haze of smoke. "Figured since you were a big-time TV star you wouldn't have time for us small-fry anymore," he said, waving the stub of his cigar at Mitchell. He squinted through the smoke.

Mitchell plopped down in the only available seat and stretched his long legs out in front of him. "I have no clue what's going on. I mean, yeah, I competed in the reality show, but I had no idea they'd started putting stuff on television. Some girl in the laundry today stopped me. I thought she was crazy. Then I get home, and I have a call

from *Live in the Morning* wanting me to come on
as a guest." He shook his head, his brow creasing
in a mixture of annoyance and amusement. He ran
his hand across his smooth scalp.

Harry tossed his head back and laughed a deep
phlegmy laugh. "Well, maybe you being famous
and all will make us famous, too. Put your face on
a poster in the window." He belly-laughed again.

Mitchell was not amused, but he couldn't help
but chuckle.

"Got you back on your same shift. That good
for you?"

"Yeah, sure. Thanks, Harry." He stood.

"Anytime. Good to have you back. I mean that."
He blew a cloud of smoke into the air.

Mitchell gave a half grin and walked out.

Before he knew it he was right back in the swing
of things, serving up drinks and chatting up the
customers. It was Alan who'd talked him into
taking that quickie bartending class and fronted
him the money. "Hey, when shit starts hitting the
fan, folks will drink," he'd said. And he'd been
right. People might not have enough money for
rent or gas, but they'd spend a few dollars to toss
one back with friends.

By seven-thirty the after-work crowd was in
full swing, almost two deep at the bar. There were

already several people waiting for tables. Blue Mondays were generally pretty busy since it was the one weeknight that dinner was half-price with two drinks, and it was blues night with a live band—hence the name. If he got a break in the action with the customers Mitchell usually sat in on a set, playing the sax. He hoped Jolene, the other bartender, would come in. Playing with the guys would sure help him unwind.

"Hey, Mitch!" a voice shouted out over the din.

Mitchell put a drink on the bar and looked up, happy to see that his friend Alan had shown up, although he couldn't quite make it to the bar. He signaled that he was going to find a seat.

It was nearly an hour later before Mitch was able to take a break and join Alan at his table.

They clapped each other on the back.

"You look rested," Alan joked. "Glad to be back?"

Mitchell looked around and slowly nodded. "Yeah, I actually am. How've things been going?"

"Busy as always. The station is starting laying off a few of the PA's, which makes everything tight. Folks actually have to do a lot of their own work," he said, chuckling.

"Hey, it's rough all over." Mitchell leaned back in his seat, then suddenly leaned forward, "Yo, let me tell you what happened today. I went to the laundry…"

He went on to tell Alan about the incident with the young woman and then coming home to the phone call from the television station, and about several comments that had been made by customers at the bar about recognizing him on television.

Alan grinned. "You be famous," he said, mockingly in ebonics. "But check this out, capitalize on it."

"What do you mean?"

"I mean, use your fifteen minutes of fame. I can hook you up on the radio as a guest, maybe get a couple of the local papers interested." His dark eyes squinted in thought. "Package you as some kind of spokesperson."

"Aw, man, come on. Me?"

"Why not? If Oprah could turn Dr. Phil into a star, and McCain could catapult Joe the Plumber into the hearts and minds of America, imagine what I can do with you."

They both hollered with laughter.

"Look," Mitchell said, still snickering, "I gotta get back on my job. We'll talk." He got up.

"I'm serious," Alan said, taking out his wallet to pay his tab. "Let me get you on the radio."

Mitchell stared at him a moment.

"Have I ever steered you wrong?"

"Well…there was that time…" Mitchell teased. "Naw, you haven't."

"All right then. I'll look at some dates and get back to you."

Mitchell nodded. "Awright. Talk to ya."

"Later, man."

"Later."

"And make sure you call the television station," Alan called out.

The following morning, after his jog, Mitchell returned the phone call to WSB-TV. He was put straight through to Deborah Myers, the *Live in the Morning* producer.

"Mr. Davenport, thank you so much for returning my call. It's always great when we have our own local celebrities. As you know, *Live in the Morning* is the highest-rated morning show across all networks. The exposure for you would be fabulous. I'd love to get you on the show to talk about your experience on the set of *Heartbreak Hotel*, what it was like being a contestant and what your plans are now."

What my plans are. Mitchell almost laughed. "I guess it would be all right. I am prohibited from talking about certain things regarding the show."

"Yes, I'm already aware of that. We've been in contact with the HH people and they're fine with you coming on. So I'd like to get you in here…for this week—Wednesday."

"Tomorrow, Wednesday?"

She laughed lightly. "Yes, tomorrow. Is that a problem?"

"Uh, no. What time do I need to be there?"

"We'll send a car for you at 5:30 a.m. I want you on during the 7:00 a.m. segment."

A car? "Sure. Fine. I'll be ready."

She verified his address and advised him not to wear anything in plaid or stripes as they tended to dance on the cameras. "Just be comfortable, whatever that is for you. We want to bring you across as that average guy. Any questions?"

"No. I think you've covered everything."

"Great. So we'll see you tomorrow. Oh, the camera crew will want to stop by your place later today to get some footage, and also Harry's Bar and Grill. We'll call first."

Mitchell hung up the phone feeling as if he was living someone else's life, because lately it sure didn't feel like his.

Chapter 20

When Sasha walked through baggage claim at Savannah International Airport the last thing she expected was to be assaulted by camera flashbulbs and a bunch of reporters shouting her name, asking for a comment.

She held up a hand to shield her eyes from the glare. *What in the world is going on?* Somehow she managed to hear April's voice over the noise and excitement. She tried to peer over heads and microphones to catch a glimpse of her friend and finally spotted her jumping up and down behind the reporters.

"Excuse me, excuse me," she said, feeling overwhelmed and a bit frightened by the attention as she tried to ease her way between the people. She made it through, stepping on a few toes in the process.

April stretched out her hand and pulled her the last couple of feet. But that didn't seem to stop the reporters. They followed her to the carousel where her luggage was.

"What is going on?" Sasha said to April as they hurried along the carpeted walkway, pursued by the dozen or so reporters.

"Clips from the show have been airing for the past week. Your face is everywhere, girl. Guess they got wind of when you were coming back."

"This is unbelievable."

April hooked her arm through Sasha's. "Just don't forget us little people," she teased. "You know you may as well make some kind of statement. They won't stop until you do."

They reached carousel three. Sasha drew in a breath, stole a strengthening look from April. She slowly turned around and held up her hand.

"I'll take two questions," she said, suddenly the consummate professional. She pressed her lips together and prayed.

"Ms. Carrington, was the relationship between you and Mitchell Davenport for real or just for the ratings?"

Sasha felt her stomach rise. Heat flooded her

cheeks. April subtly squeezed her elbow. She swallowed and ran her tongue across her lips.

"Yes," she stated simply.

"Yes, it was for real, or yes, it was for the ratings?"

"What do you think?" she tossed back with defiant assurance as the still-sore wound opened some more.

The reporters chuckled.

"Ms. Carrington, who won the competition? Can you give us a hint?"

"Sorry, you all had your two questions. Thanks." She waved, turned to the baggage carousel, saw her luggage and grabbed it.

April helped her. "Let's get out of here."

"Yes, let's."

They hurried off as the reporters called out to Sasha, and a few even followed them to the parking lot.

April got them settled in her Nissan SUV and got out of the lot as quickly as safety would allow.

Sasha was gripping the armrest for dear life. "I don't believe this." She shook her head. "The show isn't even on yet."

"Just imagine what things will be like then. Especially when everyone realizes that you won." April turned to her and grinned. "A real live celebrity."

Sasha blew out a long breath.

"Did they tell you anything before you left Antigua?"

"It was crazy when I was leaving. I thought all the interest was on the island. The producers had me sign a lot of documents—nondisclosure agreements and the land agreement and a receipt for the check. Charlotte said they would be getting in touch with me about interviews and for filming just before the show airs in two weeks. But I never expected that back there."

"Well, you know reporters, they can smell a story a mile away."

"Have you seen any of the clips?"

"Yes, chile. And you're right, Mitch is hot!" She threw Sasha a look. "Hot, you hear me? Humph!"

Sasha tugged on her bottom lip with her teeth. "I'd rather not talk about Mitchell if you don't mind," she said quietly.

"Fine. What are you going to do if he tries to contact you?"

"I thought I just asked you not to talk about him."

"I know. I heard you. But I'm just asking. What are you going to do? In a matter of days, you're going to blow up and so is he. And I know you—just because we don't talk about him doesn't mean you aren't thinking about him."

Sasha pressed her fingertips to the center of

her forehead and massaged in a slow circle. "Fine. I haven't stopped thinking about him. I keep thinking I see him everywhere I go. I dream about him. I can still feel his touch on my skin. His taste on my lips. And it's over." She turned a hard look on April, her right brow rising to punctuate her point and dared April to say anything else.

"So, can you tell me where the property is?" April asked as they headed along the highway into the suburbs of Savannah.

"You will never guess where it is."

"The Summit Hotel?" April teased.

"Ha! Very funny. No. But remember that abandoned mansion out on Route 8 just off Montgomery?"

April frowned for a moment, then her face brightened. "Yes, yes. It's huge. Was once a plantation, right?"

"That's the place."

"Oh my goodness!" she squealed. "That is incredible. Sasha...that's going to be the biggest thing to hit town since the Emancipation."

Sasha burst into giddy laughter. She hugged herself. "I still can't believe it." She shook her head in amazement, yet even as she did, in a corner of her heart her joy was tempered because she couldn't share her joy with Mitchell.

* * *

When they arrived at Sasha's apartment, April helped her in with her bags then said she had errands to run and maybe she would come back later.

As much as she loved April, Sasha was thankful for some quiet time, time to regroup and clear her head. For weeks she'd been on sensory overload.

She took her time walking around the apartment, getting reacquainted with her space. She had a ton of mail to go through and her answering machine was flashing. She was sure several of those calls were from her mother and she wasn't quite up to talking with her and explaining everything. She did, however, want to talk to her sister and let her know she was back, maybe get the inside scoop on her mother's disposition.

She got out of her travel clothes and changed into a T-shirt and a pair of cut-off shorts, something she wouldn't have dared put on a year ago. Walking barefoot on the gleaming hardwood floors, she fixed a pitcher of iced tea and took a glass with her to the bedroom where she called her sister and brought her up-to-date.

"Everyone who comes to the shop has been talking about it…and you," Tristan said. "They all want to know what happens with you and Mitchell. It's pretty clear, even from the short clips that there's something hot going on between you two."

"Hmmm. How's Mom been?" Sasha asked, steering away from where the conversation was heading.

"Fussing, of course. Wants to know why you had to sneak off. Don't even worry about her."

"I have to tell you something and you have to swear to me that you won't breathe a word of this to a soul."

"Pinky swear."

Sasha exhaled. "I won. I have my own hotel."

Tristan's ear-splitting scream jerked Sasha away from the phone. "Oh my goodness! Sasha!"

"Tris, everyone in the world is going to want to know what's going on if you don't tone it down," she scolded over a smile.

"When can you say anything?"

"Not before the show airs."

"That's what, two weeks?"

"Yes, and you better not say anything. If word gets out and back to the producers, I could lose everything. Understand?"

"Okay, okay…whew…breathe," she coached herself. "If you think Mom freaked out about you just taking a few weeks off, she is going to lose her natural mind when you tell her this."

"I know. I'll just have to cross that bridge when I come to it. Anyway, enough about me. How are you?"

"Better every day. Leaving Gary was the best thing I ever did. Some days are hard, but not as hard as living under his disrespect."

"Did I tell you how proud I am of you?"

"Nope. Ya sure didn't."

"Well, I am. I know it wasn't easy. But what I'm more proud of is that all of a sudden you were all grown up, Tris, standing on your own two feet and giving *me* advice."

"I learned from the best," she said softly.

It was good to sleep in her own bed even though she inwardly admitted that she missed hearing the sound of the ocean outside her window and walking along the beach at sunrise…with Mitchell.

She fixed an early breakfast, and, as she watched her favorite morning show from her workout on the treadmill, she nearly fell off when the host Cindy Shepherd said that coming up after the break was the first interview with one of the major contestants from the upcoming reality show *Heartbreak Hotel,* Mitchell Davenport.

She wasn't sure if her heart was ready to leap out of her chest because of the twenty-minute run on the treadmill or the shock of the announcement.

Shaking, she turned off the machine, crossed the room to the couch and sat down. Her pulse pounded so loudly in her ears that she could barely hear the introduction.

He took her breath away when the camera zoomed in on his chiseled, chocolate features. He wore a form-fitting baby-blue cotton shirt, a lightweight navy sports jacket and a pair of jeans—casually cool—and Cindy looked like she wanted to have him for breakfast.

A flash of jealousy raced through Sasha's veins as she forced herself to pay attention to the questions and not to how Cindy was constantly leaning forward and touching Mitchell's knee, practically batting her eyelashes.

"You have to tell us, Mitchell, just how real was the vibe that we all saw between you and Sasha Carrington?"

Sasha held her breath.

Mitchell grinned and Sasha felt herself get all soft inside.

"I'm pretty sure that's one of those questions I'm not supposed to answer. You'll have to watch the show and see."

"Okay, well, can you tell us, what were some of the things they had you doing during the competition?"

Mitchell gave her some tidbits about the competition, shadowing the employees and renovating the hotel.

"I want to thank you for being here with us this morning, Mitchell." Another touch on the leg. "Be sure to tune in to what is sure to be one of the biggest reality TV shows on the air, *Heartbreak Hotel,* scheduled to air right here in two weeks."

The instant the interview was over Sasha's phone rang. It was April. Then it was Tristan, both of them wanting to know if she'd watched *Live in the Morning.*

"Thanks for calling me *after* the fact," she told them both, to which they profusely apologized but both said they had been so stunned they couldn't tear their eyes away to call.

Seeing him again, and so soon, had left Sasha shaken. For the rest of the day she was completely overwhelmed with thoughts and images of Mitchell. At times she swore she could smell the scent of his skin or hear his voice whispering in her ear.

When was it going to get better? As she listened to her mother go on and on about how she was being selfish, only thinking of herself, how everyone knew what Sasha was up to except her own mother, she realized how it was going to get better. It was only going to get better is she did something about it.

The following day, bright and early, Sasha began to take the first step in her new life. She breezed through the door of the Summit Hotel, walked right past reception and a surprised-, or maybe jealous-looking Brenda, and went directly to the main office where she promptly told John Ellis that he was now her ex-boss, and she'd be curious to see how efficient the front desk would be with Brenda there full-time.

Energized and feeling suddenly free, Sasha pulled out her cell phone on the way to her car and called Misty then Tina, and asked when they would be getting into town to get started. She needed them. They both promised to be there by the end of the week once they'd made arrangements with their landlords and given notice at their jobs.

Sasha hopped in her car and headed over to her new place of business. When she pulled up in front of the ten-bedroom mansion, she sat in her car, absorbing the magnitude of what was to be the biggest step she'd ever taken in her life. Her eyes filled with tears of joy and apprehension. It was an enormous task. But she could do it.

Charlotte was due to arrive the next morning to give her the keys, take a tour and sign over the final deed to the property.

Sasha drew in a long breath and exhaled a single word…"Soon."

Chapter 21

In the days since Mitchell's television debut on *Live in the Morning,* Harry's Bar and Grill had become the place to be in Atlanta. Everyone wanted to get a picture with, shake the hand of, and in the case of the women, get to know the new local star. Harry couldn't have been happier. Business was booming, and if he had his way about it, he would have Mitchell work both the day and the night shift.

People were beginning to recognize Mitchell on the street, and he felt as though he needed a disguise to do something as simple as grocery shop at the local supermarket. If it wasn't so annoying at times, it could be funny. He actually signed autographs.

"Maybe they will be worth something one of these days," he was telling Alan as they walked down the corridor of the radio station en route to his interview.

"I'm telling you, man, you gotta milk these few minutes of fame while you can. When the show hits next week it's really going to get crazy." He patted Mitchell's shoulder. "Come on, let's get you in the booth."

"Did I tell you I got a call to do a commercial for Mercedes Benz?"

Alan grinned and clapped him hard on the back. "See, what did I tell you? Offers are going to come rolling in. What you need now is an agent," he said, bobbing his head in contemplation. He pulled open the door to the studio and introduced him to the hosts, Lisa and Jay.

"Thanks guys," Alan said on his way out. "Have a great show."

The half-hour interview was fun. Lisa and Jay did their usual bantering back and forth, tossing questions to him in between. The only sticky part came when the inevitable question was asked about him and Sasha.

"So tell us, Mitch," Lisa was saying, "were things really hot and heavy between you and Sasha or was it all show? I know we've only seen excerpts, so I can only imagine what's in store when we get the whole thing."

Mitchell had no idea whether Sasha was listening or if she even cared, but, in case she was, he wanted her to hear this from him.

"I don't know how Sasha felt, but I know what I felt was real."

"Wooo!" Lisa began fanning herself. "You heard it here first, folks. So, Mitch," she continued, leaning forward, eagerness in her eyes, "are we going to see the two of you walk off into the sunset at the end of the show?"

He chuckled. "Now, that I can't tell you. You'll have to watch."

"Fair enough," Jay said. "If you could say something to Sasha right now, what would it be?"

Mitchell cleared his throat, thought about it for a minute. "No matter where you go in life or what you do, always remember our place."

"I'm gonna faint," Lisa said dramatically. "Girls, you don't know how hot it is up this studio. Sasha, you're a lucky woman, wherever you are."

"For those of you just tuning in, we've been chatting with Mitchell Davenport, one of the contestants on the upcoming reality television show *Heartbreak Hotel.* Mitch, good luck to you and all of the ATL will be checking you out. We're going to take a break and we'll be right back."

Mitchell took off his headset and thanked his host. Lisa walked him to the door while the commercial played. She slipped her business card in his hand.

"If it doesn't work out, give me a call," she said softly, winked and returned to her seat.

Alan met him in the hallway. "Great show, my man. And while you were busy wooing the women of Atlanta I was shaping your future. I got you the name of a great agent."

"You don't waste much time, do you?"

"Hey, listen, if you're already getting offers from advertisers and anyone else, you need to make sure that your interests are covered. Not to mention that a good agent can get you work. Work equals money." He grinned.

Mitchell ran over the possibilities in his head. He'd never done television until the reality show, then his recent interview, nor had he done radio and he found he enjoyed both. He liked the excitement and the live action, definitely different from being behind the scenes of running a café. And he might be able to do the commercial for Mercedes Benz.

"Okay, let's see what your connections have to say," he finally agreed.

"I knew you would say that, so I took the liberty of setting up a lunch meeting."

* * *

When Mitchell returned to his apartment he was prepped to be a new client of Steele-Perkins Management. They handled television, commercials, voice-overs and film. Jake Steele had promised to get a contract over for him to sign the following day, and had made him promise to forward any inquiries directly to the agency. He said he knew the people running the Mercedes commercial and would give them a call when he returned to the office.

Life had done a complete one-eighty. Mitchell was feeling optimistic, good about himself and the future. The days ahead might not be what he'd originally envisioned for himself, it looked like they'd be better.

As he put his key in the door he heard the phone ringing. Tossing his knapsack on the chair he crossed the short space to the wall phone in the kitchen.

"Hello?"

"Hi, Mitch, it's Regina."

It was the first time that Sasha had been out on the town since her return. She'd put on a simple eggshell-white camisole top with a cropped sweater of the same color, a pair of linen pants and open-toed sandals with a kitten heel. She'd piled her hair on top of her head in a loose chignon. She felt every bit the star that strangers were making her out to be. Amazing how she'd gone from nearly in-visible not only in her family but in every aspect of her life to *this*.

It totally tickled April and Tristan how many people recognized Sasha from the clips of the show as the three of them walked from April's car to the restaurant.

"If you give me a few dollars I can be your body guard," April teased.

"No, silly, *we're* the entourage. You know how stars always have a crew," Tristan corrected, and they all laughed.

"You two are ridiculous. It's not that serious," Sasha said, although she was thrilled by the attention.

Sasha, April and Tristan were shown to a table near the window of their favorite restaurant. They ordered mimosas for starters.

"I know you heard what he said on the radio today," Tristan began.

"I heard him." Sasha turned her water glass around in a small circle on the linen-topped table.

"And?" April prodded.

"And what? What am I supposed to do? Go running after him?"

"Yes!" they said in unison.

"Before someone else does," Tristan added, thinking of her own failed marriage.

When Sasha had heard Mitchell say that what

he felt for her was real, live on national radio, *elation* could not describe her emotions. All the doubts that she'd had since they'd parted disappeared. She had hope again that somehow, someway, they could work things out, and that she wasn't alone in how she felt. But as the day wore on, doubt began to rear its ugly head. So much of television and radio is to titillate the audience. Maybe his "confession" was all for show.

"Why don't you give him a call?" April suggested.

Sasha slowly shook her head. "No. He'll think I'm…"

"You're what…in love with him? Would that be so bad?" Tristan pressed.

Sasha's soft features pinched. "I just can't. That's all."

Mitchell knew he shouldn't be doing this. Going to Regina's apartment was a mistake. But even as he walked down the pathway to the front of her complex he understood that he had no other choice.

When she'd called earlier, she'd sounded contrite, sincere, soft and crazy sexy. She said she needed to talk. There was so much she wanted to tell him, to explain to him. Would he come over later? It wouldn't take long, she'd promised.

So here he was. At least he had the option of

walking out rather than having to put her out if the need arose. He rang her bell and waited, his hands jammed into the pockets of his jeans.

Moments later the door opened. For an instant, he felt that old pang in the center of his chest. There was no debating the fact that Regina Patterson was stunning by anyone's standards. Luminous soft-brown eyes that tipped slightly up at the corners, a testament to her mixed African-American and Asian ancestry. Inky-black hair that fell like a veil to her shoulder, sweeping dark brows and full luscious lips. She was petite, barely five foot five, but with the body of a goddess, and she had no problems showing it off, which she did now in a form-fitting honey-toned outfit that was so close to her skin color that she looked naked.

A seductive smile moved slowly across her mouth and darkened her eyes. "Mitchell," she breathed. She extended her hand to him and pulled him inside. "Thank you for coming," she said, leaving a trail of something soft and inviting in her wake. "I fixed us something to eat. I wasn't sure if…anyway, let me know if you're hungry," she said, sounding uncharacteristically nervous.

Mitchell looked around. The apartment definitely had Regina's touches, from the art on the walls to the light-colored accessories and bold-colored flowers. Several of her photography pieces that he remembered from when they'd lived together were mounted on the walls as well.

"Nice place."

"Thanks. Please, have a seat."

"I really can't stay long, Gina. I have to be at work in an hour. What did you want to talk to me about?"

"I wanted to talk about us."

He managed a sardonic grin. "There is no us, remember?"

At least she had the decency to look guilty, he thought.

"And that's my fault. I was selfish and scared and I didn't think about how much you needed me to be there for you."

"Now you do, I suppose."

She blinked, glanced away, then back at him. She lifted her chin a notch. "I was wrong, Mitchell. I haven't stopped thinking about you and what we had together. I want that again, if you'll just give me a chance. I know I can make you happy." She got up from her seat and sat next to him. She looked deep into his eyes. "Don't you remember how it was between us?" she asked on a breath, pressing her lips to his neck.

He turned his head away. "Yes, I remember." He extricated himself from her and stood. He looked down into her startled expression. "I remember it all, Gina. But you know what I remember the most? I remember you walking out and saying that you couldn't be with a loser. That it wasn't what you signed on for. Remember? For months I couldn't get you out of my mind. I kept hearing those words over and over from the woman who was supposed to love me. You have any idea what that does to a person?"

"Mitch…" she pleaded, reaching for him.

"Don't!" he barked. "It's over, Gina. For good. If you left me once, what's to stop you from leaving again? That's not love, that's opportunity. And if there is one thing that you were always good at it's seeing and seizing an opportunity." He gave a crooked smile. "And you smell an opportunity now." He stared at her for a long moment, memorizing the stunned look in her eyes before letting out a breath of relief and moving toward the door. "Opportunity has just left the building." He opened the door and walked out, closing it softly behind him.

As he drove toward Harry's he felt something he had not felt in a very long time—closure, and the weight of self-doubt was completely lifted from his soul. He'd needed to confront Regina, look her in the eyes and let her know that it was over—for him, for good. She'd be pissed, but she'd get over it. If nothing else, Regina Patterson was a survivor.

He turned on the radio, cranked it up and sang along with Leela James's version of "A Change Is Gonna Come." Oh yes, it is.

Chapter 22

The premiere of *Heartbreak Hotel* was the most highly rated reality television show of all time. Pre-publicity and major media blitzes were responsible for its enormous success. Across the country there were watch parties, with everyone rooting for their favorite teams.

Over the next six weeks the anticipation leading up to the finale intensified. Everywhere you went, people were talking about the competition, and Mitchell and Sasha in particular. They were both now full-blown celebrities and Mitchell's larger-than-life billboard ads for Mercedes Benz and his television commercial upped his celebrity. The advertising slogan, "Better than reality television," became the phrase of the day.

When he got his first check from the billboard ad, Mitchell couldn't believe the number of zeros, but that was nothing compared to the check from the television commercial. "And you'll be getting checks for as long as that ad runs," his agent assured him.

On the night of the finale, when Sasha had to let the world know what her decision was, hearts broke all over the country when they heard her poignant confession and discovered that Mitchell, rather than force her to make a choice, had taken himself out of the equation so that she could have her dream and win the prize of a lifetime.

Now that's true love, women were saying to their boyfriends and husbands late into the night. Mitchell was an instant hero and Sasha was the woman that every woman wanted to be.

His agent's phone hadn't stopped ringing since the show premiered, but Mitchell's big break came after the finale. He'd been offered a small part on one of the daytime soaps and he was going to have to fly out to New York for a reading and screen test.

"This is major," Jake was saying. "Look at John Stamos, he started out on the soaps. And George Clooney made his mark on *ER*."

"How soon would I have to go?"

"The sooner the better, but I can probably stretch it out for a week or so. No more."

"I'll call you."

"Do that. And Mitch…"

"Yeah…"

"Congratulations, my man. The sky is the limit."

Everywhere that she looked, she saw him—on billboards dotting the highways and on her television screen. She was filled with a kind of happiness that was hard to explain. She knew how much Mitchell needed a new start for his life and she was thrilled that such incredible opportunities had come his way. But she wondered if it was what he wanted or if he was simply going along for the ride. Deep down in his heart he wanted something to call his own. And as wonderful as all the fame and celebrity was, it wasn't his dream.

There wasn't a day that went by that she didn't think of him, and when it got really hard, she would take a drive, park on the road and look up at his picture, gorgeous and smiling, leaning casually against a gleaming Mercedes… "Better than reality television. Ain't nothing like the real thing," she would whisper.

Preparations for the grand opening of her hotel—which she'd named Epiphany, were well underway and it was only a matter of weeks before she would welcome her first guests. The waiting list was already months long. The staff had been hired and Misty and Tina were managing the day-to-operations. All of her supplies had been delivered, and the minor repairs that the building needed had been completed. She was giddy with excitement, bone-weary from all the work, yet there was a place inside her soul that was empty.

The day before the grand opening, Sasha sent everyone home so that they could arrive in the morning fresh and ready to face the guests and the cameras, and then she took a final look around.

As she went from room to room, floor to floor, checking and rechecking, she was overcome with tears of pride. She'd done it. She'd actually done it.

All her life she'd played second fiddle, stayed in the background, never thinking that her life could ever be more than what it was. Even her own mother had wanted to keep her in her place and she was still having a hard time accepting that Sasha wasn't going to be around at her beck and call anymore. She had a life of her own. And with her holistic approach to her establishment—she united aesthetics with nutrition and relaxation therapy—she hoped to start a new trend in resorts.

She took a final look around before preparing to leave. When she stepped outside, the sun was just beginning to set, and the humidity from earlier in the day was easing. Tomorrow was the first day of the rest of her new life, she thought as she slowly walked down the pathway toward her car. She looked out onto the road and saw a car pull up and hoped that it wasn't some news-hungry reporter ready to waylay her at the last minute. She picked up her step just as the car door opened, and then she froze with the keys in her hand.

She'd know that walk anywhere, slow, panther-like and controlled, a sensuousness that was barely contained. Her heart thudded. Her stomach curled into a tight knot. And then he was there right in front of her. It wasn't a billboard or an image on the television screen.

Her eyes danced over his face before she reached out and touched his cheek to assure herself that he was real and not the work of her overactive imagination and starving body. Her gasp was audible in the still of the night when the warmth of his chocolate-brown skin played against her fingertips.

He grasped her hand and pressed it to his face before covering her palm with kisses.

Her body trembled when his arm snaked around her waist and pulled her close.

"I haven't stopped thinking about you," he whispered, inches away from her lips, before his covered hers in a kiss that exploded like fireworks.

Sasha melted into him, clinging to the hard lines of his body, her soft moans captured within his kisses.

Suddenly he lifted her off her feet and spun her around in a circle as they both roared with delight before setting her down again.

She looked up at him. "What are you doing here?" she asked breathlessly, clasping his hands in hers.

"So much has happened. So many things have changed."

A raindrop popped on Sasha's nose and then another. They both glanced up to see the storm clouds moving overhead. Before they could react the sky opened up and they made a mad dash for the mansion. Sasha fumbled with the key and finally got the door open and them inside.

They fell into each others arms laughing and dripping-wet.

"Well I have plenty of towels," she said, turning on the lights.

Mitchell looked around in amazement. The entryway was gleaming in the tradition of the antebellum mansions—cathedral ceilings, sparkling wood floors, marble and stone pillars and seating around the bay windows with a magnificent chandelier as a centerpiece.

"How many rooms?" he asked, wiping water from his face.

"There are ten bedrooms, each with its own bath. There is a pool out back and the basement has been turned into my relaxation center—massage and aroma therapy, sauna and exercise room. Out back is a pond filled with koi." She took him on a tour and got them both towels from the supply room.

Thunder rumbled overhead as lightning lit up the heavens. The lights flickered.

"The main dining room is this way." She led him past the reception desk to the left and opened the double doors. Circular tables to accommodate around forty people dotted the room that looked out over the pond. "We also have a smaller dining room on the other side for private parties."

"Amazing. You've done an incredible job."

"Fortunately it didn't need the kind of work that the place in Antigua did."

They both groaned at the memory.

"And if for some reason they need a change of scenery there's a new restaurant and jazz club opening up down the road."

She turned to him, exhaled the breath she'd held. She was greeted by his smile of pride and joy for her. "You've been busy, too," she said, feeling the heat rising between them.

"I had to leave," he said, steering the conversation in a new direction.

She swallowed.

"I couldn't put you in the position of having to choose. I know how hard you worked, and how much you wanted this. And if there was any chance that you felt about me the way I felt—and feel—about you… I just couldn't do it."

"That's why I fell in love with you," she softly admitted.

Mitchell's eyes sparkled.

"From the moment we met, no matter what roadblock I threw in your way, you still thought of me first and what I needed, what would be best for me."

He cupped her face in his hands. "I didn't want to be the prize you chose by default. I wanted to be all the man you needed and deserved and I knew I could never be that until I found a way to reclaim my life on my own terms. Now I have."

Her heart bumped in her chest.

"The money from the commercials and the ads gave me the financial foundation that I needed to start over. Remember that café that I told you I wanted one day?"

She nodded, not knowing where this was heading.

"It's under construction and I'll be ready to move into my new house in about a month." He paused. "And I want you to be a part of my life. I want to be able to take care of you, let you fill all the empty spaces."

Fear gripped her. "But…how can I leave my business, my home, and come with you to Atlanta?"

A wicked grin lit his face. "Oh, I guess I forgot to tell you—that restaurant and jazz club that you mentioned? That's mine." Sasha's mouth opened but no words came out. He took her hand and walked her to the window. He pointed to the two-story house down the road, barely visible under a cloud-covered rainy sky.

"What?" She looked at him in confusion. "That's the house I've wanted to live in since I was a little girl. But someone bought it right out from under me."

"I remember you told me about it the first night we met." He leaned down and kissed her, deep and slow, before leaning back to look into her eyes. "Now you can live in it. With me. If it's what you want."

"I…what…"

He nodded. "Marry me, Sasha. Let's build a world, a life together. Me and you."

Tears sprung into her eyes. Her throat was so tight with emotion that she could barely get out the words. "There's nothing I'd rather do," she said, her voice breaking with emotion.

Mitchell swept her up into his arms, cradling her like a baby against him. "I love you," he murmured against her soft lips.

"I know." She sighed.

A gleam lit his eyes. "Bedrooms upstairs?"

She giggled. "Yes."

"Let's christen one of them tonight."

She cuddled closer as he mounted the stairs and walked down the hallway. He opened the door to the first bedroom, crossed the space and laid her down on the bed.

"We're going to have to get the room back in order before the staff and the guests and the cameras get here in the morning," Sasha said as she pulled his shirt over his head and took off her own.

He unbuttoned his pants and kicked them off, sat beside her on the bed and unhooked her bra. Before she could take a breath he suckled one of her nipples, and she whimpered in delight.

Mitchell groaned deep in his throat when she stroked him, her fingers velvety soft and sure. Unable to contain his need for her a second longer, her pushed up her skirt, pulled her panties off and moved between her legs.

The hot, wet contact was electric. They both shuddered in unison as Mitchell moved deep inside her, slow and steady, finding his way back home.

"Better than reality television," Sasha moaned, knowing that this, having Mitchell in her life, was the true prize of a lifetime.

* * * * *

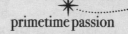

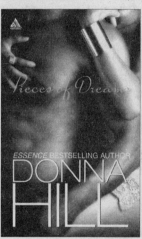

HOLLINGTON HOMECOMING

Where old friends reunite...
and new passions take flight.

Book #1 by Sandra Kitt
RSVP WITH LOVE
September 2009

Book #2 by Jacquelin Thomas
TEACH ME TONIGHT
October 2009

Book #3 by Pamela Yaye
PASSION OVERTIME
November 2009

Book #4 by Adrianne Byrd
TENDER TO HIS TOUCH
December 2009

Ten Years. Eight Grads. One weekend.
The homecoming of a lifetime.

REQUEST YOUR FREE BOOKS!

2 FREE NOVELS
PLUS 2 FREE GIFTS!

KIMANI™
ROMANCE

Love's ultimate destination!

HELP CELEBRATE
ARABESQUE'S
15TH ANNIVERSARY!

2009 marks Arabesque's 15th anniversary!

Help us celebrate by telling us about your most special memories and moments with Arabesque books. Entries will be judged by the Arabesque Anniversary Committee based on which are the most touching and well written. Fifteen lucky winners will receive as a prize a full-grain leather duffel bag with the Arabesque anniversary logo.

How to Enter: To enter, hand-print (or type) on an 8 ½" x 11" plain piece of paper your full name, mailing address, telephone number and a description of your most special memories and moments with Arabesque books (in two hundred [200] words or less) and send it to "Arabesque 15th Anniversary Contest 20901"—in the U.S.: Kimani Press, 233 Broadway, Suite 1001, New York, NY 10279, or in Canada: 225 Duncan Mill Road, Don Mills, ON M3B 3K9. No other method of entry will be accepted. The contest begins on July 1, 2009, and ends on December 31, 2009. Entries must be postmarked by December 31, 2009, and received by January 8, 2010. A copy of these Official Rules is available online at www.myspace.com/kimanipress, or to obtain a copy of these Official Rules (prior to November 30, 2009), send a self-addressed, stamped envelope (postage not required from residents of VT) to "Arabesque 15th Anniversary Contest 20901 Rules," 225 Duncan Mill Road, Don Mills, ON M3B 3K9. Limit one (1) entry per person. If more than one (1) entry is received from the same person, only the first eligible entry submitted will be considered. By entering the contest, entrants agree to be bound by these Official Rules and the decisions of Harlequin Enterprises Limited (the "Sponsor"), which are final and binding.

NO PURCHASE NECESSARY. Open to legal residents of U.S. and Canada (except Quebec) who have reached the age of majority at time of entry. Void where prohibited by law. Approximate retail value of each prize: $131.00 (USD).

VISIT **WWW.MYSPACE.COM/KIMANIPRESS**
FOR THE COMPLETE OFFICIAL RULES

KP15ARACONTEST